And that was when he saw her.

The woman with the most amazing hair: dark as midnight, flowing down almost to her waist, perfectly straight and shiny. She was wearing a short scarlet dress that set her hair off to perfection and showcased long, beautifully shaped legs. And somehow she was managing to salsa in a pair of seriously high heels.

Aaron blew out a breath. This wasn't why he was here. He wasn't looking for any kind of relationship right now, even a temporary one. Not when he was about to start a new job and all his time was going to be taken up with work.

Yet there was something about the woman that drew him.

As he watched her dance she turned slightly and he saw her face properly for the first time. She was stunning, with a heart-shaped face, dark eyes and the most beautiful mouth he'd ever seen.

Her friend said something to her and she tipped her head back and laughed, revealing even white teeth.

Aaron forgot all about why he was here. Forgot about everything except the woman in the red dress. Instead of being the staid, sensible workaholic he'd always been, he found himself walking across the dance floor towards her. Moth to a flame.

And, right at that moment, he didn't care if he got burned.

Dear Reader

This book actually started life about five years ago, when the late author Maggie Kingsley and I were chatting about how interesting it would be to have a shaman as a hero.

I haven't gone quite that far in this book—my heroine is the daughter of an American Indian healer—but I did enjoy the research. And, given that my heroine has been wrapped in cotton wool for her entire life, it makes sense for her to want to work in an area where she gets to do exciting things vicariously, through her patients—hence she works in the department of tropical medicine and infectious diseases.

Then there's my poor hero, from a family who doesn't just have a stiff upper lip—they're practically encased in permafrost. When he ends up falling for my heroine, who has a close family which adores her, he's like a fish out of water. How is he going to learn to cope with it and get a happy ending?

You'll have to read on to find out :) And I hope you enjoy their journey.

I'm always delighted to hear from readers, so do come and visit me at www.katehardy.com

With love

Kate Hardy

IT STARTED WITH NO STRINGS...

BY
KATE HARDY

® and TM are trademarks owned and used by the
trademark owner and/or its licensee. Trademarks
marked with ® are registered with the United Kingdom
Patent Office and/or the Office for Harmonisation in the
Internal Market and in other countries.

First published in Great Britain 2014
by Mills & Boon, an imprint of Harlequin (UK) Limited,
Large Print edition 2015
Eton House, 18-24 Paradise Road,
Richmond, Surrey, TW9 1SR

© 2014 Pamela Brooks

ISBN: 978-0-263-25468-6

Harlequin (UK) Limited's policy is to use papers that
are natural, renewable and recyclable products and made
from wood grown in sustainable forests. The logging
and manufacturing processes conform to the legal
environmental regulations of the country of origin.

Printed and bound in Great Britain
by CPI Antony Rowe, Chippenham, Wiltshire

Kate Hardy lives in Norwich, in the east of England, with her husband, two young children, one bouncy spaniel and too many books to count! When she's not busy writing romance or researching local history she helps out at her children's schools. She also loves cooking—spot the recipes sneaked into her books! (They're also on her website, along with extracts and stories behind the books.) Writing for Mills & Boon® has been a dream come true for Kate—something she wanted to do ever since she was twelve. She's been writing Medical Romances™ for over ten years now. She says it's the best of both worlds, because she gets to learn lots of new things when she's researching the background to a book: add a touch of passion, drama and danger, a new gorgeous hero every time, and it's the perfect job!

Kate's always delighted to hear from readers, so do drop in to her website at www.katehardy.com

Recent titles by Kate Hardy:

Mills & Boon® Medical Romance™

200 HARLEY STREET: THE SOLDIER PRINCE*
HER REAL FAMILY CHRISTMAS
A DATE WITH THE ICE PRINCESS
THE BROODING DOC'S REDEMPTION
ONCE A PLAYBOY…
DR CINDERELLA'S MIDNIGHT FLING
ITALIAN DOCTOR, NO STRINGS ATTACHED

200 Harley Street

Mills & Boon® Cherish™

BEHIND THE FILM STAR'S SMILE
BOUND BY A BABY
BALLROOM TO BRIDE AND GROOM

Dedication

To Penni Askew and Scarlet Wilson,
with love—and thanks for the encouragement!

Praise for
Kate Hardy:

BOUND BY A BABY
won the 2014 RoNA
(Romantic Novelists' Association) Rose award!

'BOUND BY A BABY moved me to tears
many times. It is a full-on emotional drama.
Author Kate Hardy brought this tale
shimmering with emotions.
Highly recommended for all lovers of romance.'
—*Contemporary Romance Reviews*

'When you pick up a romance novel
by Kate Hardy you know that you're going to be
reading a spellbinding novel which
you will want to devour in a single sitting
and A CHRISTMAS KNIGHT
is certainly no exception.'
—*CataRomance*

CHAPTER ONE

'WELCOME TO LONDON.' Aaron lifted his pint in a wry toast to himself.

It was his own fault that he was sitting here on his own at the bar in a salsa club. When Tim had suggested going out to celebrate Aaron's first weekend in London and catch up, of course he hadn't meant just going out for a quiet pint. Aaron should've remembered their student days: Tim had always been the life and soul of the party, and always ended up surrounded by a crowd of pretty girls. He was still the same in his thirties as he'd been in his late teens; right now, Aaron couldn't even see him in the crowded club.

So when he'd finished his pint, Aaron decided, he'd try and find Tim, say a quiet goodbye, and go back to the impersonal flat he'd rented near the hospital.

Or maybe he wouldn't even bother with the rest of the pint. He set the still half-full glass back on the bar and turned away, looking for Tim.

And that was when he saw her.

The woman with the most amazing hair: dark as midnight, flowing down almost to her waist, perfectly straight and shiny. She was wearing a short scarlet dress that set her hair off to perfection and showcased long, beautifully shaped legs. And somehow she was managing to salsa in a pair of seriously high heels.

Aaron blew out a breath. This wasn't why he was here. He wasn't looking for any kind of relationship right now, even a temporary one. Not when he was about to start a new job and all his time was going to be taken up with work.

Yet there was something about the woman that drew him.

As he watched her dance, she turned slightly and he saw her face properly for the first time. She was stunning, with a heart-shaped face, dark eyes and the most beautiful mouth he'd ever seen.

Her friend said something to her and she tipped her head back and laughed, revealing even white teeth.

Aaron forgot all about Tim. Forgot why he was here. Forgot about everything except the woman in the red dress. Instead of being the staid, sensible workaholic he'd always been, he found himself walking across the dance floor towards her. Moth to a flame.

And, right at that moment, he didn't care if he got burned.

'You are the best friend *ever*.' Joni hugged Bailey. 'And I love you.'

'I love you, too, sweetie.' Bailey hugged her right back.

'You were so right. Dancing and champagne. That's just what I need tonight.' It was pretty much what Joni had originally planned to be doing tonight—except it would've been a different sort of dancing. A slow, elegant waltz in a floaty, frothy bridal dress to a romantic song; whereas right now the dancing was hot, sweaty, endorphin-boosting salsa and the dress she was wearing had the shortest skirt she'd ever owned, thanks to Bailey's encouragement.

'Of course I'm right. I'm a doctor,' Bailey teased. 'And exercise is one of the best medicines ever.'

Joni laughed. 'Says the specialist in sports medicine who's just a teensy bit biased.'

'It's true. I can quote tons of studies.' Bailey spread her hands. 'There are links to reduction in the risk of cancer and dementia, it works as well as drugs in curing depression, and it boosts academic progress in teenagers. Wins all round.'

'So salsa's the cure for everything?' Even a broken heart? Though Joni didn't quite understand why her heart should still feel broken when she'd been the one to call off the wedding, six months before.

'Endorphins rock. Plus salsa's fun.' Bailey grinned. 'Now, *shimmy*!'

Joni couldn't help laughing. And trust her irrepressible best friend to stop her moping on the day she'd been dreading for months: the day of the wedding-that-wasn't. Bailey specialised in sports medicine and Joni in tropical and infectious diseases; but even though they didn't actually work together they'd been best friends ever since they'd met on their first day at university. They'd supported each other through the dark times and celebrated the bright ones.

'Don't look round,' Bailey said, 'but there's a hot guy who was sitting at the bar. Right now he's heading in our direction, and he's looking straight at you.'

'He's probably wondering what on earth someone as coordinated as you is doing dancing with someone who keeps doing the steps totally wrong,' Joni said with a smile.

'I don't think so. Try "wow, who's the hot babe?" Especially as your hair's down.' Bailey wound the end of Joni's hair briefly round her fingertips. 'You know, every woman in this room would kill for your hair. Including me.'

Hair that Marty had wanted her to cut. Her ex was the latest in a string of men who'd made Joni feel that she wasn't quite good enough. And she'd vowed after Marty that she'd never make that mistake again—she wouldn't sacrifice her career or her self-esteem just to please someone else. From now on, it was equal or nothing.

'Earth to Joni.' Bailey waved both hands in front of her face. 'We agreed. No brooding and absolutely no thinking about Marty the Maggot. And I think Hot Guy is about to ask you to dance.'

Joni shook her head. 'Even if he does—'

'Then you're going to say yes,' Bailey cut in. 'Doctor's orders. Dancing with a hot guy is good for you.'

'So if he asks *you* to dance—' Joni began.

'He's not going to ask me, sweetie.' Bailey winked at her. 'He's only got eyes for you.'

Aaron stood close enough that she'd be able to hear him over the music, but not close enough to be creepy. 'Would you like to dance?' he asked.

'I, um…'

The blush made her look even prettier. And he liked the fact that she clearly wasn't aware of how gorgeous she was.

Even though his head told him this was insane, the rest of him most definitely wasn't listening. And then her friend smiled and said, 'Dancing's a great idea. My feet are feeling a bit sore right now and I really need to sit down for a few minutes.'

Aaron knew she was fibbing, because she'd been dancing without even the slightest wince as he'd walked over to them, but he appreciated her tact.

'Bailey!' There was the tiniest hint of panic in Ms Drop Dead Gorgeous's eyes as her friend waved and did a theatrical limp in the direction of the chairs at the bar.

Yeah. There was a fair bit of panic going on inside him, too, right now. He knew from experience that getting involved was a bad idea—emotions just led to pain—but he'd asked her to dance and it was too late to go back. Too late for doubts.

'Hello. I'm Aaron,' he said, extending a hand.

'I'm Joni.' She took his hand and shook it nervously. 'Look, I'm sorry about my friend. I—'

'There's no need to apologise,' he said with a

smile. 'Though I might have to apologise to you in advance, as I'm not exactly the world's best dancer.'

'Neither am I. Bailey's the one who can dance, not me,' she said ruefully. 'Though I'll try not to tread on your feet.'

'Let's make that a mutual pact,' he said, and took her hand to dance with her.

Somehow, they muddled through the first half of the next track together; then the awkwardness between them seemed to vanish and the panic seeped away. And Aaron found himself really enjoying the throbbing Latin beat of the music.

Especially when the next song came on and everything slowed down. And then she was in his arms, right where he wanted her to be, all warm and soft and sweet. They swayed together, moving in time to the music; his arms were wrapped round her waist and her arms were wrapped round his neck.

He smiled down at her. Her dark eyes were gorgeous; up close, he could see that she wasn't wearing much make-up. She didn't need it. Just the tiniest bit of mascara to emphasise those long, long lashes, and soft red lipstick that made him want to kiss it all off. Even as the thought went through his head, he found himself dipping his head down towards hers. When his mouth brushed against hers, it felt like electricity prickling through every nerve end. Then she kissed him back, and the rest of the room seemed to vanish; there was only the two of them and the music.

But the next track was one with a much faster beat, and they were forced to pull apart. They stood there, just looking at each other, and Aaron wondered if Joni felt as dazed as he did.

This really shouldn't be happening. He didn't do this sort of thing.

And yet…

'Hey. I'm going to get a taxi home,' her friend said as she joined them.

'I guess I'd better go, too,' Joni said.

But Aaron wasn't ready to let her go. Not yet. 'Stay just a little bit longer?' he asked. 'I'll make sure you get home safely.'

* * *

Bailey leaned in closer so that her mouth was hidden from view and her words were for Joni's ears only. 'Stay and have some fun,' she said. 'Don't start thinking or analysing.' She squeezed Joni's hand. 'Just enjoy it for what it is: a bit of a dance with a seriously hot guy. And, before you ask, no, your lipstick isn't all over your face— even though you were snogging like teenagers just now.'

Joni felt the colour flood through her skin. 'Oh, God. I'm behaving like a tart,' she muttered.

'No, you're not. You're just having some fun on a night that would've been difficult for you otherwise. Nothing serious, no consequences. Just live for the moment and enjoy it. And, actually, snogging Hot Guy there will be very good for you. It'll produce more endorphins. We like endorphins. Endorphins are *good*.'

Trust Bailey to take that tack. Joni couldn't help smiling. 'Are you sure you don't want me to come with you?'

'I'm sure,' Bailey confirmed. 'Stay and have some fun. Call me tomorrow, OK?'

'I will.' Joni hugged her goodbye, then carried on dancing with Aaron until her feet were sore.

'Shall we have a break and get a drink?' she suggested.

'Great idea,' he said.

She liked the way he walked with her towards the bar, with a hand protectively at her back and yet not making her feel helpless and pathetic, the way her exes had always ended up making her feel. Aaron had beautiful manners, and he didn't seem the sort who would put a woman down to make himself feel better. Not that she trusted her own judgement on that score any more. She'd got it wrong so many times in the past, thanks to the rose-tinted glasses she couldn't seem to remove.

'My shout,' she said as they reached the bar. 'Bailey and I were drinking champagne, earlier. Would you like to join me?'

'Are you celebrating something?' he asked.

She certainly was. The luckiest escape of her life. Though, at the same time, part of her mourned the wreckage of her future plans. It should've been so good…

For a second Joni looked sad, and then Aaron wondered if it had just been his imagination because she gave him a broad, broad smile. 'It's Saturday night, and that's always worth celebrating, isn't it?'

He had a feeling that she didn't mean anything like that at all, but he didn't push her to elaborate. He simply smiled and accepted the glass of champagne she'd offered.

Then they danced until most people had either drifted home or gone elsewhere, and the dance floor was almost empty. Aaron noticed that Tim hadn't bothered trying to find him or say goodnight when he left. But that was Tim all over—a good-time guy who didn't think too deeply. Maybe he ought to take a leaf out of his old friend's book.

And he wasn't quite ready to see Joni home just yet.

'There probably aren't any cafés open nearby,

so would you like to come back to my place for a coffee?' he asked.

She looked wary. 'Thanks for the offer, but—'

'Hey,' he cut in softly, 'when I said coffee, I meant *just* coffee. I'm not expecting anything else.'

She bit her lip. 'Sorry, I'm not used to…well…'

She had to be kidding. That gorgeous, and she didn't date?

Or maybe she'd just come out of a relationship, one that had left her confidence shaky. Making him Rebound Man. Which was fine, because that meant she wouldn't want forever from him. 'It's OK,' he said. 'Me, neither.' He didn't date much. In between work, studying, work and more work, he simply didn't have time.

Wanting to lighten the atmosphere, he said, 'Though I can tell you that my coffee-making skills are a lot better than my dancing.' He'd worked as a barista to help put himself through university, and his expensive Italian coffee machine was the one gadget he'd never part with.

'Then thank you,' she said. 'I'd love a coffee.'

As they left the club, they were lucky enough to see an empty taxi passing. He hailed the cab, gave the driver his address, and held the door open for her to get in.

Joni was quiet in the back of the cab and Aaron didn't push her to talk; he simply curled his fingers round hers, and eventually the pressure was returned.

How long was it since he'd held hands with someone in the back of a taxi?

He reminded himself not to think. This relationship wasn't going anywhere. This was just for tonight; he didn't do 'for always'. Never had and never would.

When the taxi stopped outside his flat, he paid the driver and ushered her across to his front door.

She removed her shoes as soon as they were inside the front door. 'Um, may I borrow your bathroom, please?'

'Sure.' He indicated the bathroom door. 'I'll be through here in the kitchen when you're ready.'

She was a while in the bathroom. When she joined him in the kitchen, she said, 'Can I be immensely rude and cheeky and ask for a glass of orange juice and a sandwich as well as the coffee, please?'

Oh, help. He'd come across this before. Someone who was suddenly hungry and thirsty after going clubbing and then going to the bathroom. If he looked closer, he'd just bet her pupils would be pinpoints.

His thoughts must have shown in his face because she said, 'Actually, yes, a needle was involved.'

Uh-oh.

'But not drugs,' she said crisply.

'Not drugs.' He really wasn't following.

She took something out of her bag to show him. 'I'm a diabetic and this is a blood glucose monitor. I prick my finger and test the blood on a strip to check my blood sugar levels. Right now, my blood sugar's a bit out of whack—probably because I had a couple of glasses of champagne tonight and I don't usually drink very much, plus I've spent all night dancing. So right now I could do with some carbs to get my blood sugar stable. I'm not going to pass out on you or anything like that,' she reassured him swiftly. 'This just happens sometimes, and a sandwich and some orange juice will sort me out pretty quickly.'

He relaxed, then. Diabetes explained a lot. Joni might still be trouble with a capital T, but at least it wasn't going to get complicated and he wouldn't feel responsible for someone else making a bad lifestyle choice. And clearly Joni was very used to looking after herself properly because she'd explained exactly why her blood sugar was a problem right now and how it could be fixed.

He almost told her he was a doctor, but he didn't want to make her feel awkward. Instead, he poured a glass of juice and handed it to her.

'Thank you.'

He rummaged in the fridge. It had been years since he'd done a stint on the endocrine ward, but he remembered that a protein and carbohy-drate snack was good for someone whose blood sugar was a bit low but not in the unmanageable range. 'Would a bacon sandwich be OK?' he asked. And please don't let him have offended her because she was a vegetarian. He'd already made enough of an idiot of himself.

'A bacon sandwich would be absolutely fantastic. Thank you so much.' She gave him another of those sweet, sweet smiles. 'Is there anything I can do to help?'

'No, it's fine. You can sit and chat to me, if you like.'

He put bacon under the grill and grabbed the bread, then turned to face her. 'What kind of coffee would you like? Cappuccino, latte, flat white?'

She looked surprised. 'You can really do all those sorts of coffees?'

He gestured to his coffee machine. 'Yup. My one bit of self-indulgence.'

'Impressive.' She smiled. 'A cappuccino would be lovely—but no chocolate on the top for me, please.'

'You don't like chocolate? Or is that a diabetic thing?'

'A bit of both,' she said. 'I'm probably the only woman in the world who doesn't really like chocolate. My best friend says I'm weird.'

He laughed, and made her a cappuccino.

She took a sip and her eyes widened. 'This is fabulous. What coffee do you use?'

'It's a blend from a deli in Manchester,' he explained. 'I'm hoping I'll find somewhere like it in London.'

'So you've just moved here?'

He nodded. 'I'm starting a new job.' Moving on. Moving upwards. Making a difference. The one thing he hadn't been able to do when it really counted, and he'd vowed to spend the rest of his life making up for it. Not that he wanted to talk about why he'd always been so driven in his career. Especially to someone he'd only just met. So he concentrated on making them both a bacon sandwich, then handed a plate to her.

She took a bite. 'You are *perfect*.' Then she blushed. 'Sorry.'

Aaron couldn't resist teasing her. 'Were you talking to me or the sandwich?'

'The sandwich,' she confessed. 'Though I guess that, as you made it, you're perfect by association.' She grimaced. 'Sorry, my social skills are usually a bit better than this. Blame it on the champagne.'

'No problem.' He smiled at her. He couldn't remember the last time he'd met someone so cute; her warmth and sweetness made him like her instinctively.

And that made Joni exactly the wrong kind of woman for him. The more he talked to her, the more he could tell that she wasn't the sort who kept relationships short and sweet and didn't let them get in the way of her life, the way he did. He didn't want something permanent—and it wouldn't be fair to lead her on and let her think that he could offer her something he knew he just wasn't capable of giving.

He managed to make small talk until she'd finished her coffee. 'I'll drive you home.'

She looked nervous. 'That's very nice of you to offer, but you were drinking at the club.'

'I had half a pint of beer, plus one glass of champagne with you, and we've just eaten. I'm safely under the alcohol limit for driving, but I can call you a taxi if you'd rather.'

'Thank you, but I think I've impinged enough on you. I'll call one myself.'

He knew he should just let her go—it would

be the sensible option. But something made him want to keep her close, just for a last few moments.

'Dance with me again first?' he asked.

She looked at him. For a moment he thought she was going to say no; then she nodded. 'OK.'

He put on an album by a jazz singer with a soft, smoky voice and held out his arms. She walked into them and rested her head against his shoulder. He rested his cheek against her hair; it was as soft and silky against his skin as he'd expected it to be.

This was a bad, bad idea.

But he couldn't help himself. There was just something about her. Something different. Something that drew him. Something he couldn't put his finger on.

As they swayed together, he gave in and closed his eyes, letting himself focus on holding her and dancing with her.

He wasn't sure which of them moved first, but then he was kissing her—*really* kissing her— and she was kissing him all the way back.

He dragged his mouth from hers. 'Joni,' he whispered.

She stroked his face, and he ended up pressing a kiss into her palm. 'I honestly didn't ask you back here for anything more than coffee.'

'I know,' she said softly.

He was finding it hard to breathe. 'But now… Will you stay?' he asked, his voice hoarse.

CHAPTER TWO

WOULD SHE STAY or would she go?

Aaron didn't have a clue.

Joni was silent for a long, long time. And then she said, 'I, um, don't usually do this sort of thing.'

'I'd already guessed that,' he said softly. 'Sorry. I shouldn't have asked you.'

'It's not that,' she said. 'I'm flattered. But I'm not looking for a relationship right now.'

'Neither am I,' he said. 'Which makes it even more unforgivable of me to have asked you to stay. It's totally dishonourable.'

He was about to turn away and grab the phone to call her a taxi when she slid her hand over his and squeezed it. 'The answer's yes.'

He knew he ought to give her a chance to change her mind. But right now he wanted this so badly. *Needed* this so badly. And he had the strongest feeling it was the same for her.

In answer, he kissed her.

Then he lifted her up and carried her to his bedroom. He stood by the bed and let her slide down his body so she was left in no doubt about how much he wanted her.

She looked him in the eye and licked her lower lip.

He took the invitation and kissed her, then lifted her hair so it fell over her shoulder towards the front of her body, turned her round and undid the zip very, very slowly. He caressed her skin as he uncovered it; it was so soft, he couldn't resist touching his mouth to it and kissing his way down her spine. She made a tiny noise of pleasure, so he unsnapped her bra and continued kissing his way downwards. When he eased the dress over her shoulders so it could slide to the floor, she stepped out of it. Then, once he'd dealt with her bra, he turned her to face him.

'You're so beautiful,' he said softly. She was still wearing her knickers and, with her hair falling to cover her breasts, she looked almost as modest as she would've done wearing a bikini at a beach. Yet, at the same time, she was sexy as hell. The ultimate temptress.

'I need to see you, Joni,' he said hoarsely. 'Lift your hair.'

Just as he'd hoped, she pushed her hair back with both hands and lifted them to the back of her head.

'Like a goddess,' he whispered.

She blushed. 'Hardly. I'm just an ordinary woman.'

Did she really have no idea? 'You're gorgeous,' he said. 'Everything about you. Your hair, your smile, your eyes—just gorgeous.'

This time, she actually smiled. 'And I'm feeling just a little bit vulnerable here, because you're wearing an awful lot more than I am.'

It took him less than ten seconds to get naked. 'Better?'

'Much better.' And this time it was his turn to blush as she surveyed him.

She leaned forward and traced a line from his ribcage to his belly button. 'Very nice abs.'

'Thank you. But I'm just ord—' He caught himself as she laughed.

'You're not very good at taking compliments,' she said.

'That makes two of us,' he said wryly.

She swallowed. 'I forgot to ask—do you have, um, protection?'

'Yeah. Though I guess I ought to check it's in date.'

She blinked. 'You're seriously telling me that a hot guy like you…' She stopped and clapped her hand over her mouth. 'Sorry. None of my business. No questions.'

Meaning, he thought, that she didn't want him to ask questions, either. That moment when she'd looked sad in the salsa club and then claimed that she was celebrating… Whatever the reason, she clearly didn't want to talk about it.

And it suited him just fine—because he didn't want to talk about emotional stuff, either.

'Thank you for the compliment,' he said, focusing on the bit that wasn't going to rake across any raw edges. 'I guess I ought to let you know that I don't normally invite women I've only just met back to my flat.' He stroked her face. 'And I'm pretty sure you don't normally accept invitations from men you've only just met.'

'I don't.' She shook her head.

So why him? Why tonight?

No questions.

Ask nothing, and you'll hear no lies. And you won't be expected to answer anything, either, he reminded himself.

He rummaged in his bedside drawer and checked the date on the packet of condoms. 'We're safe.' He paused. 'Though if you'd rather I left the room so you could get dressed while I call you a taxi, that's fine—I'm not the kind of man who'd ever force a woman to do something she didn't want to do.'

'I know,' she said softly. 'Or I wouldn't have agreed to come here with you.'

Funny how her confidence in him warmed him. It almost felt as if something had cracked around the region of his heart. Though he was pretty sure the permafrost would be too deep for that. This was about pleasure, not emotions. He'd make this good for her. Good for himself, too. And then he'd drive her home, they'd say goodbye, and the chances of their paths crossing again in a city of nearly eight million people were pretty remote. They'd just get on with their lives. And he could go back to doing what he always did: getting on just fine with people, fitting in with the crowd on the surface, and not letting himself get too close to anyone.

'Don't think,' she said softly.

Meaning that she didn't want to think, either? He was pretty sure that she was running from something; and he appreciated that she didn't want to discuss it. Because he sure as hell didn't want to discuss what was ricocheting round his head.

'No thinking,' he agreed, and kissed her.

And it was easier not to think when he was touching her. Easier just to feel, to lose himself in pleasure.

He pushed the duvet aside, then lifted her up and laid her against the pillows.

She stroked his cheek and smiled at him. 'Aaron.'

He kissed her again, then hooked his thumbs

into the sides of her knickers and drew them down. She lifted her bottom slightly so he could remove them easily.

'You're beautiful,' he said again. 'And I really want to touch you.'

'Then do it,' she commanded softly.

He dipped his head and nuzzled the hollows of her collar bones. She arched back against the bed and he moved lower, taking one nipple into his mouth and sucking hard. She slid her hands into his hair, urging him on.

He kissed his way down over her abdomen, then shifted to kneel between her legs. She dragged in a breath as he took one ankle and slowly stroked his way upwards, letting his mouth follow the path of his fingers; and she was almost hyperventilating when he kissed his way along her inner thigh. Which was just what he wanted; right now he wanted to make them both forget everything except this.

'Aaron, yes,' she whispered as his tongue stroked along her sex.

He teased her, flicking the tip of her clitoris with the tip of his tongue, taking it harder and faster until she was almost whimpering in need, then slowing it right down again and letting it build up and up again. He could feel the second that she climaxed, her body tightening beneath his mouth; he held her there for a long, glorious moment, and then ripped open the foil packet, slid on the condom, and pushed into her.

He could still feel the aftershocks of her climax rippling through her. He loved the idea that he'd managed to turn this gorgeous woman to complete mush.

'Aaron,' she whispered, and he held still, letting her body adjust to the feel of him inside her.

'I wanted the first time to be for you,' he said softly.

Her eyes filled with tears, as if she wasn't used to being considered like that, and he wanted to punch the guy who'd made her think her feelings weren't important. Right at that moment he had a pretty good idea what she'd been running from and why her confidence in herself was so low.

Well, he could make her feel better. And at the same time he could make himself feel better, too.

'No thinking,' he said, and began to move.

She wrapped her legs round him to draw him deeper and tensed her muscles round him.

'That's so good,' he groaned.

She smiled, and did it again.

'Do you know what I really want?' he asked.

'What?'

'You on top of me. With that glorious hair falling over both of us.'

She looked slightly shocked. 'You like my hair?'

How could she not know how glorious her hair was? 'I *love* your hair.'

She smiled, and let him roll with her so that he was lying on his back and she was straddling him. Then she moved over him and tipped her head forward so her hair fell over them, just as he'd asked.

And the reality was even better than his fantasy.

'You're gorgeous,' he said. 'Totally gorgeous.'

She seemed to like being the one in control; she teased him the way he'd teased her earlier, letting the pressure build to almost fever pitch and then easing off just a little, then letting it build again.

By the time he climaxed, he was near to hyperventilating.

He felt her hit the peak again at the same time, so he wrapped his arms round her and held her tightly until it had all ebbed away.

'I'd better deal with the condom,' he said finally.

She nodded. 'And I guess I ought to get dressed and call a cab.'

He glanced at his bedside clock. 'At this time of the morning?'

She looked at the time, too, and grimaced. 'I suppose it's a little late.'

'Stay,' he said softly. 'No pressure. Unless you have to be somewhere?'

'I can be anywhere I choose,' she said.

'Then stay,' he said, shocking himself. What the hell was he doing? He should be getting dressed and offering to drive her home, not asking her to stay. This was the first step on a very slippery slope towards letting someone into his life. Bad move. He was rubbish at being close to people. Work was fine, but anything emotional made him back off. Every single one of his girlfriends had complained that they needed more emotional commitment than Aaron could give them. But not one of them had made him feel strongly enough to want to change or keep the relationship going—and that reinforced what he'd always known, deep down. Love wasn't for him.

So he needed to stop this. Right now.

But his mouth clearly wasn't working with the plan. 'I can make you breakfast. There's a patisserie round the corner that does fantastic croissants.'

'And would that mean more of your coffee?' she asked.

'Definitely more of my coffee.'

Where was his common sense? Why wasn't he pushing her out of here as quickly as he could?

He made a last-ditch effort to put an obstacle in the way. 'Do you need—well, insulin or anything?'

'I'm sorted,' she said.

He could hardly say now that he'd changed his mind and ask her to leave, could he?

OK. This was just for tonight. Spending one night with someone wasn't the same as a declaration of everlasting love, was it? So it wasn't as if he was going to screw things up totally. Even he couldn't manage to do that with a one-night fling.

He went to the bathroom, dealt with the condom and came back to the bedroom. 'There are fresh towels in the bathroom. Help yourself to whatever you need.'

She gave him an embarrassed smile. 'I know this is going to sound crazy after what we've just done, but do you, um, have a bathrobe or something I could borrow?'

'Sure.' He took his bathroom from the hook behind the door and handed it to her. 'And I'll close my eyes.'

'Thank you.'

She returned a few minutes later, smelling of his citrus shower gel and with her skin still slightly damp.

'Do you want me to close my eyes again?' he asked when she stood beside the bed.

She nodded. 'It's a bit pathetic, I know.'

No. It just meant she really wasn't used to having a one-night fling.

But maybe this was what both of them needed, right now.

He waited until she'd got into bed and he'd felt the duvet being pulled up on her side, then leaned over and kissed the tip of her nose. 'Just for the record, it's not pathetic,' he said. 'It's kind of cute. And I'm very flattered that you chose me to—um, well. Be with you.'

'Hmm,' she said, but her eyes crinkled at the corners.

'Let's get some sleep,' he said, and switched off the light.

It had been a long, long time since he'd spent the night with someone. He knew it wasn't the most sensible decision he'd ever made; but right now it felt good to fall asleep curled round a warm body. So he'd go with it. And tomorrow— tomorrow, they'd have breakfast, they'd smile, they'd say goodbye and they'd walk away.

* * *

Joni was warm and comfortable, the body wrapped round hers holding her close.

Then she opened her eyes as the realisation hit her. *The body wrapped round hers.*

She'd stayed overnight with Aaron.

Uh-oh.

This could be awkward.

Last night was—well, last night. A crazy impulse, one she really shouldn't have acted on.

Why had she stayed for that last dance? Why had she let him kiss her stupid and then made love with him? Why hadn't she taken the chances he'd offered her to back away and flee to the safety of her own flat?

Panic seeped through her. What would Aaron expect of her this morning? Last night he'd talked about having breakfast. But would he think that they were now officially a couple because she'd stayed the night? Or would he, too, be having these doubts and panicking that she'd want much more from him than he was prepared to give?

She took a deep breath, held it, and listened.

He was breathing deeply and evenly. OK, so he could be faking it—but his body didn't feel tense against hers, which it would do if he really was faking it, Joni told herself. His body felt relaxed; so it was pretty safe to assume that he was still asleep, and she might just have a chance of salvaging the situation.

Leaving without saying goodbye was taking the coward's way out, she knew, but right at that moment she could live with that. All she had to do was get out of the bed without waking him, collect her clothes, dress as quickly as she could, and then let herself quietly out of his flat and out of his life. The chances of them bumping into each other again in a city as big as London were pretty remote, especially as she had no intention of going back to the salsa club. And this way they'd both be left with some good memories and no disappointed expectations.

Tentatively, she lifted the fingers of his hand away from her waist. His breathing remained deep and even, to her relief. Clearly Aaron was one of those people who slept like the dead and it would take a really loud alarm to wake him in the morning.

She hoped.

Moving slowly, she managed to wriggle out of his hold and slide out of the bed.

There was enough light coming through the curtains for her to locate her clothes, and she remembered that she'd left her shoes by the front door. She crept out of the room, hoping that she wouldn't accidentally stand on a squeaky floorboard and wake him, and closed the door very gently behind her.

From there, it was a matter of seconds to drag her clothes on and find her handbag where she'd left it on the worktop in his kitchen.

Leaving without a word seemed a little harsh. But there was a memo block and a pen next to the phone in his kitchen. She scribbled a brief note and left it pinned down in the corner by one of the clean mugs. Then she collected her shoes and let herself quietly out of his flat.

A passer-by in the street gave her a knowing look; it was Sunday morning, and she was dressed for a Saturday night, so it was obvious that she hadn't gone back to her own place. She ignored the passer-by and straightened her spine. OK, so her behaviour last night hadn't been the way she normally acted. But it had been exactly what she'd needed. Aaron, unlike Marty, had made her feel good about herself. He'd taken away the lingering sadness of a day she'd been dreading. So she had no regrets. And now she'd find a taxi, go home, and get on with the rest of her life.

Aaron woke to find the bed beside him stone cold.

Joni had clearly left without waking him.

He knew he ought to feel relieved; he really didn't want the complication of getting involved with someone. And yet he was shocked to discover that what he actually felt was disappointment. He'd actually been looking forward to waking up beside Joni and having a leisurely breakfast together.

Was he totally crazy?

He shook his head to clear it. He knew nothing about Joni other than her first name. The chances of finding her in a city like London were next to nothing. And that, he reminded himself sharply, was probably for the best.

He showered, dressed, and went to make himself a coffee. Which was when he saw her note: *Thank you for everything. J.*

Cute. Good manners.

But he also noticed that she hadn't left him her phone number or any way of contacting her. Which meant that, as far as she was concerned, last night had been a total one-off. She didn't want to see him again.

'It's for the best,' he said—out loud, this time, to convince himself properly. Though his voice sounded a little bit hollow.

Still, he didn't have time to brood. He started his new job tomorrow. And that would keep him busy enough to stop him thinking about the gorgeous woman with amazing hair who'd made him see stars and spent the night curled in his arms.

New job. New responsibilities. Part of a new team.

And on his own. Which was the only way that really worked for him.

CHAPTER THREE

'So HAVE YOU met our new consultant?' Nancy, the ward sister, asked as Joni made herself a coffee in the ward kitchen.

'Not yet. I've been in the travel medicine clinic all morning, and this is the first break I've had today,' Joni said. 'What's he like?'

'Here he is now, so you can take a look for yourself,' Nancy said as the door opened.

Joni turned towards the newcomer, all ready to be friendly and welcoming to a new colleague— then looked at his face and stopped dead.

Of all the wards, in all the hospitals, in all the world, he had to walk into hers.

She could see the immediate recognition in his face, too.

Oh, great. The one and only time in her life when she had a mad, crazy fling with a handsome stranger, and he turned out to be someone who was going to be working with her for the foreseeable future.

How come life ended up being this complicated and awkward?

Eric Flinders, the head of the department, introduced them. 'This is Mr Hughes, our new consultant—Aaron, you've already met Sister Meadows. This is Dr Parker, our specialty reg. She's going to be working closely with you.'

Awkwarder and awkwarder. If only the ground would open and swallow her now, she thought.

But it didn't.

She had no choice but to face him.

'Mr Hughes. Very nice to meet you,' Joni said politely, and held her hand out to him.

To her relief, he didn't mention that they'd met before and simply shook her hand. 'Nice to meet you, too, Dr Parker.'

So much for never seeing his beautiful stranger again, Aaron thought. And now he'd just been told that he was going to be working closely with her.

The high heels, short skirt and amazing hair

of Saturday night were all gone. Today, she was wearing trousers and a white coat, teamed with flat shoes, and her hair was neatly plaited into a single braid.

And he also noticed that there was a name tag on her coat. Dr N. Parker. And yet she'd called herself 'Joni' on Saturday night. It didn't stack up. Had the name she'd used been an extra layer of disguise?

She was smiling, but the smile didn't quite reach her eyes. It wasn't lack of friendliness he saw there, though, but sheer unadulterated panic. Clearly she was worrying that he was going to mention Saturday night.

Well, he wasn't going to tell any tales if she didn't. Because this was just as awkward for him as it was for her. Saturday night had been a moment of craziness; the last thing he wanted right now was to start a new relationship. And he really, really hoped it was the same for her.

'You'll be doing the TB clinic together this afternoon,' Eric Flinders said. He smiled at Joni. 'Perhaps you'd like to brief Mr Hughes on the clinic and how things work around here?'

'Of course, Mr Flinders,' she said.

So they worked on formal terms in the department? Aaron wondered. Or was it just Eric Flinders who insisted on formality?

Joni glanced at her watch. 'Um, perhaps I could brief you over lunch, Mr Hughes?'

'That works for me, Dr Parker,' he said with a smile.

She returned his smile. 'Good, because then I can show you where the cafeteria is and what have you. A new hospital always feels a bit like a rabbit warren until you get to know where everything is, doesn't it?'

Now he understood why the head of the department had asked his junior colleague to do the briefing rather than doing it himself. Joni Parker was clearly the sort who took new people under her wing and made them feel part of the team. Which meant she was a sweetheart, as well as being utterly gorgeous. And that made her even more off limits, as far as Aaron was concerned.

'Thank you,' he said politely.

'I'm actually due on ward rounds now,' she

said. 'So shall I meet you here at half past twelve?'

'Half past twelve will be fine,' he said. And the frightening thing was that he was actually looking forward to it. Hell. He had to stop this. Right now. Joni—Dr N. Parker—was his colleague first, last and everything in between. And he'd better keep that in mind.

She was ten minutes late meeting him. 'I'm so sorry. The ward round took a bit longer than I th—'

'That's fine,' he cut in gently. 'I know we have targets for treatment times, but if a patient needs a bit of extra time you can't just tell them they've already had their allotted few minutes and they'll just have to wait for the next appointment.'

She shot him a grateful glance. 'Thanks for understanding. I guess we ought to head to the cafeteria right now, or we'll be late for the TB clinic this afternoon. I'm really sorry to cut your lunch break short.'

'It's not a problem,' he said.

It would've taken him twice as long to find

the place without her showing him the way, Aaron thought as they reached the hospital café. He wasn't surprised when Joni chose a super-healthy balanced meal rather than grabbing the nearest sandwich and a chocolate bar, and she was drinking plain water rather than a sugary drink; she was clearly very careful about her blood sugar. Saturday night really had been out of the norm for her, then.

And he really had to stop thinking about Saturday night. About how her skin had felt against his. Any relationship with her other than a working one was completely out of the question.

'The coffee here isn't too bad,' she said—and then blushed, as if remembering the coffee he'd made her. 'Um. Anyway. I guess our ward works the same as wherever you were before.'

'Manchester.'

'OK.' She smiled at him. 'So we have the usual ward work and ward rounds, referral meetings, case reviews and research meetings. Then we have the regular clinics—TB, travel medicine, parasitology and general tropical diseases. There's also a daily walk-in clinic for people who've just come back from abroad, so they don't have to be referred by their GP first. That one tends to be the usual stuff—tummy bugs, rashes and fever. Sometimes we have something a bit rarer, but for the most part it's gastro symptoms.'

Pretty much what he'd done in Manchester. Though he noticed that Joni went through the entire run-through without actually looking him in the eye. Which didn't leave him much choice; he was going to have to broach the subject, and they were going to have to deal with it and get it out of the way.

'Dr Parker,' he said softly.

She looked nervous. 'Ye-es.'

'It might be a good idea if we dealt with the elephant in the room.'

She blew out a breath. 'I'm sorry. I don't usually…' She buried her face in her hands. 'Arrgh. I said I'd stop apologising all the time, too. Bailey would fine me for that one.'

He knew who Bailey was—the friend who'd been at the salsa club with her—but he really didn't follow the rest of it. 'Fine you? Why?'

'For apologising when I don't need to.' She gave him a wry smile. 'You know how people sometimes have a swear jar if they're trying to give up swearing, and they put money in it every time they swear? Well, I have a sorry jar. I'm banned from using the s-word more than once a day.' She bit her lip. 'And I bet I've apologised to you twice already today.'

'Try three.' He just about managed to hide a grin. 'I won't tell if you won't,' he said. 'And, actually, that was what I was going to say. No telling. What happened at the weekend is just between us and has nothing to do with anyone else.'

'Thank you.' She looked relieved. 'I couldn't believe it when I saw you. I mean, in a city the size of London—what are the chances of even bumping into you again, let alone finding out that we're working together?'

'Pretty small,' he agreed. 'Though I guess, given what we both do for a living, we would've met again at some point—maybe through a friend of a friend of a friend.'

'It's not even as if infectious and tropical diseases is a common speciality,' she protested.

'True. But I bet you know everyone in the emergency department.'

'I guess I do,' she admitted. 'If we haven't worked together on a case, we've met at an inter-departmental do.'

'As I said. Friend of a friend of a friend.' He shrugged. 'Maybe we should start again, as if we've just met for the first time. Hello. I'm Aaron Hughes, tropical medical specialist. Pleased to meet you.' He held out his hand.

She shook it, and his skin tingled where she'd touched him. Not good. He really didn't want to react to her like this. He couldn't afford any emotional ties.

'I'm Joni Parker. Also a tropical medical specialist. Pleased to meet you,' she said.

So she'd been telling the truth about her name on Saturday, then. But 'Joni' didn't start with N, and he was curious. He glanced at her name tag. 'What does the N stand for?'

'Nizhoni,' she said. 'But my first name's a bit

of a mouthful, so people tend to call me Joni for short.'

'It's an unusual name,' he remarked. Not one he'd ever heard before.

She nodded. 'It's a bit exotic.'

'I guess it goes with your speciality. Also exotic,' he said. 'And now I'm going to shut up before I dig myself another hole.'

'I can't argue with that. And thank you. For not—well—making a big deal out of it.' She rewarded him with a real smile. One that made those gorgeous dark eyes light up—and that, in turn, made his blood tingle. Which was a seriously bad idea. He couldn't afford to let himself get emotionally involved with Joni Parker, no matter how attractive he found her. He'd learned at a young age that keeping his distance was the safe way. The way not to get hurt. Loving someone just led to loss and heartbreak. Keeping your distance was the only way to survive with your heart intact.

'I guess we both acted out of character,' he said. 'And now we're colleagues. Making a big deal out of what happened is going to make work awkward.'

'Which is the last thing you need, especially in a new job.'

'Exactly. And I'm sure you could do without it, too. So today's the first time we met, OK?'

'OK,' she agreed.

'I think the only difference between here and Manchester,' he said, 'is that everyone's more formal here. I'm used to working on first-name terms with my colleagues.'

'We do here, too,' she said. 'Except for Mr Flinders—he's a bit of a stickler for formality.'

'So it's first-name terms most of the time, and formal around the head of department?' Aaron asked.

'Pretty much,' she said. 'Nancy's lovely—she's the senior sister. Most of the team's been here longer than I have, but we've got a couple of others just started—there's Mikey, our F1 doctor, who's not sure if he wants to do tropical medicine or emergency for his specialty, so he's doing a six-month rotation with us to help him make his mind up, and two newly qualified nurses.'

She filled him in on the rest of the team. 'Actually, we're a fairly close bunch. We try to get a team night out at least once a month. We take turns in organising it, and there's a bit of a competition about who can find the most unusual thing to do.' She gave him the most mischievous grin. 'I win, at the moment.'

'What did you do?' he asked, intrigued.

'Pizza night,' she said.

'And that's unusual *how* exactly?' he asked, not understanding in the slightest. There was practically a pizzeria on every street.

Her grin broadened. 'It's unusual if you have to walk through a rainstorm without getting wet first.'

He looked at her, understanding even less. 'How does that work? You're telling me you can predict the weather?'

She took pity on him. 'No, it was an art installation. It's finished now, or I'd suggest you go, because it was utterly brilliant and I went four times. Basically there were sensors that picked up your movements and stopped the "rain" falling on you. Though that depended on how you moved and how quickly you moved.'

'That sounds like fun,' he said.

'It was. We were like a bunch of kids, trying to get the sensors to rain on us. We tried hopping through the room, waltzing, moonwalking, doing the samba...' She laughed, and again Aaron felt his blood heat. Hell. Get with the programme, he reminded his head. She's off limits.

'We've done ice-skating, had a tango lesson— oh, and there's always food afterwards, whether it's fish and chips or pizza or a curry. And then there's the quarterly quiz night with the emergency department. The losing team keeps the winners in chocolate biscuits for a week. I hope you're good at general knowledge, because we lost the last three.' She gave him another of those mischievous grins that made him want to pull her into his arms and kiss her. 'We could really do with a win this time, just to stop them gloating quite so much.'

'I'm reasonable at general knowledge, but don't bet the biscuits on me,' he said, returning the grin. 'It's nice that you're close to other departments.'

'We are.' She sighed. 'But the new hospital director doesn't quite see it like that. He's sending a group of us on a team-building exercise in a couple of weeks, to one of those outdoor course places.'

'It sounds as if you don't approve,' he remarked.

'I think we do a good enough job on our own. If we really need expert help in building a relationship with our colleagues in other departments, that'd make us a pretty sad bunch. And if we really have to have the experts in, then I'd rather get someone to come in for a morning to do a team-building thing in one of the hospital meeting rooms, and spend the rest of the money on the patients, rather than spend all that cash sending teams of staff out to some expensive place.' She shrugged. 'But it's not my call and I guess we have to do what the hospital director says.'

'I guess,' he said. 'Can I buy you a coffee?'

She looked wary. 'Why?'

'Just to say thank you for showing me around and telling me pretty much everything I need to know about how the department works,' he added swiftly.

She smiled, looking relieved; Joni Parker really was an open book, Aaron thought. What you saw was exactly what you got. Clearly she wasn't used to hiding her emotions, the way he was.

'You really don't have to—I'm always happy to show people round—but thank you, a coffee would be lovely. Cappuccino, please, but no chocolate on the top.'

Yeah. He remembered. And he was glad of the excuse to leave their table before he did something reckless. Like asking her out to dinner. Because that would be a really stupid thing to do. They were colleagues. They didn't need complications like being attracted to each other. Even if she was the most gorgeous woman he'd ever met. He needed to resist these wild, utterly ridiculous urges.

He had to hide a grimace when he brought their coffee back to their table and took a sip of his espresso. And for once he clearly wasn't that successful in hiding his thoughts because she said, 'You hate it, don't you?'

'I'm a bit of a coffee geek,' he said. 'So I'm not answering that one.'

She smiled. 'In that case, I should warn you that the stuff in the ward kitchen is instant, and it's not that posh barista-style instant coffee either. It's whatever happens to be on special offer in the supermarket when Nancy takes the kitty and tops us up on tea and coffee. And the tea's usually worse than the coffee.'

'Warning heeded,' he said.

'So how did you get to be a coffee geek?'

It was a personal question, but not an emotional one, so he didn't mind answering. 'I worked as a barista while I was a student. And it was at an indie coffee house, not a chain. My boss was a super-geek—the coffee equivalent of a wine buff. I learned a lot from him.'

'Hence your posh coffee machine.' Joni blushed. 'Um. The one I'm only guessing about, that is. I wouldn't know anything about your kitchen.'

He couldn't help smiling. 'Of course.'

She glanced at her watch. 'We'd better go. Clinic's in fifteen minutes.'

A convenient excuse, he thought. And one that suited him, too. Because he'd discovered that the more time he spent with Joni Parker, the more he liked her. Which wasn't what was supposed to happen. And it could be seriously dangerous to his peace of mind.

Bailey had called Aaron 'Hot Guy' at the salsa club. But at the hospital Aaron was even more gorgeous, Joni thought. She'd always had a soft spot for geeky guys—she would've picked Clark Kent over Superman any day—and, in his white coat and with those narrow-rimmed glasses, Aaron would definitely count as geeky.

Though he was also way, way out of her league.

So remembering the way he'd made her feel on Saturday night was totally stupid. He'd been the one to bring up the subject in the hospital cafeteria, and he'd made it very clear that he had no intention of repeating what had happened be-tween them. And she knew he was making the right call: any kind of relationship between colleagues who worked together, apart from a professional one, could make life way too awkward for the rest of the team.

It would be much more sensible to keep her distance.

And she'd focus on being professional.

Their third patient in the TB clinic that afternoon was a nineteen-year-old girl who'd taken a gap year before starting university and had worked at a school in Borneo.

'I've been home a couple of months,' Cara said, 'but for the last month I've been coughing a lot. I've tried about ten different sorts of cough mixture but none of them works and I just can't get rid of it.' She bit her lip. 'Then last week I started coughing up icky stuff, and there was blood in it. I panicked a bit and Mum dragged me off to the family doctor. He…' She caught her breath. 'Mum looked it up on the Internet. It's a sign of cancer. And so's losing weight without trying. And I've been really hot and sweaty at night.'

'Have you been eating normally?' Joni asked, thinking about the weight loss.

'I haven't been feeling that hungry,' Cara admitted. 'And I'm tired all the time. Mum says that's a symptom of cancer, too.'

'Losing your appetite and being tired can be symptoms of a lot of other things, not just cancer,' Aaron said gently, reaching out to take her hand. 'It's good that the Internet is making people aware of their health, but sometimes you can really scare yourself with what you read, so it's always a good idea to go and check with your doctor to stop yourself worrying unnecessarily.'

'The doctor sent me for an X-ray. I think he thought it might be cancer, too.' She shivered. 'I'm nineteen. I'm too young for this.'

'As Mr Hughes said, there could be lots of things causing your symptoms,' Joni said gently. 'Your family doctor sent you for that X-ray so he could start to rule things out, not because he was sure it was cancer. And I can tell you that as a doctor I normally start by ruling out the nasty stuff, because I don't want my patients worrying any longer than they need to.'

Cara nodded. 'The guy who did the X-ray said there weren't any signs of a tumour. But he said there were white patches on my lungs and it might be TB.'

'That's why he sent you to us for the next lot of tests—TB comes under tropical medicine and infectious diseases,' Joni explained.

Aaron brought up the X-ray file and turned the screen so Cara could see it, too. 'There is some scarring on your lungs, here and here, and those white patches are a classic symptom of TB. Plus you mentioned those other symptoms—night sweats, loss of appetite and losing weight. That's all adding up to a picture for me.' He looked at the screen. 'I see that your family doctor also sent you for a skin test.'

'Last week.' She frowned. 'But I don't see how it can be TB. I don't even know anyone who's ever had TB. I mean, I didn't think people even got it any more. How could I get it?'

'TB is a bacterial infection, and it's still pretty prevalent in parts of the world,' Aaron explained. 'It's spread by droplets—coughs, sneezes, that sort of thing. It can affect the lungs, which is why it makes people cough and why your doctor sent you for an X-ray to check your lungs, but it can also affect other parts of the body. That's why we need to check you out here. Not everyone who has TB is infectious, so you won't catch it by just sitting next to someone on a train—but if you share a room with someone who has TB then there's much more of a chance of you picking it up. And you said you've spent a few months in Borneo, yes?'

She nodded. 'Three months, working as a teacher.'

'Borneo has quite a high rate of infection, so if your skin test is positive then I'd guess that's where you picked it up.'

Cara looked worried. 'I shared a room with some of the other students working out there. Does that mean they might be infected, too?'

'Either one of them infected you, or if you picked it up from somewhere else then you might have infected them,' Joni said. 'So it would be a good idea to get in touch with them and ask them to go and see their doctor to get themselves checked out.'

'I don't have everyone's number,' Cara said. 'But I can call the agency that did the placements and ask them to pass on an urgent message to everyone.' She bit her lip. 'Oh, God. I feel so bad that I might've passed this on to other people.'

'It's not your fault,' Joni said. 'You didn't know you were ill, and TB takes a while to show up.'

'So you had the skin test on Friday?' Aaron asked, double-checking her notes. At Cara's nod, he examined her lower arm. 'There's definitely a hard red lump there, so the skin test is positive.' He measured the lump and Joni updated Cara's notes with the details. 'I'll need you to do a sputum test for me as well, but we have to culture the bacteria so it'll take a couple of weeks to get the results back.'

'So what happens while we wait for the results?' Cara asked.

'I'm pretty sure from the results of the skin test, plus what I can see on the X-ray and the symptoms you've described, that you have TB. So I'd like to start treatment now,' Aaron said.

'The good news is that you can be treated at home—you don't have to stay in hospital,' Joni added, seeing the flicker of dread on Cara's face. 'We'll give you a course of antibiotics. You need to take two different types to make sure the infection clears up.'

'You'll start to feel better after a couple of weeks,' Aaron said, 'but it's really important for you to keep taking the medication for the next six months and don't stop taking it just because you're feeling better.'

'Six months?' Cara looked shocked.

'Six months,' Aaron confirmed. 'Otherwise the infection won't clear up and the bacteria might become resistant to the antibiotics we give you. If that happens, it will take even longer to clear up.'

'OK. I promise I'll take the medication, even after I feel better,' Cara said.

'Good. Sometimes people get side effects from the antibiotics,' Joni told her. 'If you do, you need to come back and see us so we can change the medication you're on to something that will deal with the TB but won't give you the side effects.'

'So that's if you feel nauseous or you're actually sick, if you get a rash or itching, or you have any numbness or tingling in your hands or feet,' Aaron said. 'And I'd want you to come straight back and see us if your skin goes a bit yellow and your urine's dark, or you start getting blurred vision.'

Cara looked worried. 'Blurred vision?'

'It's one side effect, but we can sort it out. I know it's a lot to take in, but we'll give you a leaflet with all this information so you can talk it over with your mum,' Joni said. 'As well as a leaflet with advice on how to stop TB spreading to your family, friends or anyone you're in contact with at work or college. You need to cover your mouth when you cough or sneeze or laugh, and put any used tissues in a sealed plastic bag. And don't sleep in the same room as anyone else, as you might cough or sneeze in your sleep.'

'Because that's how it spreads,' Cara said.

'Exactly. For now, you need to stay at home—we'll see you once a fortnight and keep an eye on you, and we'll tell you when it's safe to go back to work or college,' Aaron said. 'If you're worried at any time, just come and see us or give us a call.' He wrote the prescription while

Joni printed off the patient information notes for Cara.

He was good with patients, Joni thought. Clear and thorough—and kind, too, like the way he'd squeezed the girl's hand to reassure her through her worries about cancer. And the way he worked so easily with her made the clinic a pleasure. This was teamwork at its best. She had no intention of jeopardising that with a ridiculous crush on the guy. Give it a few days and it would go away anyway.

She hoped.

The clinic was soon over, leaving them both with notes to write up.

'Thanks for making my first clinic here a good one,' he said.

'Pleasure.' Had it not been for Saturday night, she would've invited him out for a drink with a couple of the others after the end of their shift tonight or tomorrow, to help him settle in. But Saturday night *had* happened; and she didn't want him to take any invitation the wrong way, especially as he'd made it very clear that he didn't want to take up where they'd left off.

So the attraction wasn't mutual—and Joni wasn't going to start yet another relationship with a man who'd make her put most of the effort in. Been there, done that, and finally learned her lesson. 'I guess I'll see you tomorrow, then.'

'Sure. See you tomorrow,' he said, and left for his office.

CHAPTER FOUR

'YOU'RE KIDDING. MR HOT from the salsa club is your new consultant?' Bailey whispered from her yoga mat as the class moved into the downward dog position.

'Yup.' Joni groaned softly. 'And it gets worse.'

'Jenna's glaring at us, so we'd better stop talking. Tell me after class and get in the plank position,' Bailey whispered back.

'I hate the plank,' Joni said feelingly, but did it anyway.

After the yoga class, they went to the bistro round the corner.

'Two glasses of sparkling water with a slice of lime, please, two chicken superfood salads,' Joni said to the waitress, 'and please can we swap the dough sticks—?'

'For extra avocado? Sure. I'll bring them right over,' the waitress said.

Bailey smiled at her best friend. 'Now we've hit thirty, we're so predictable that the staff here know exactly what we're going to order even before we look at the menu.'

'Though we have actually tried everything on the menu here,' Joni reminded her. 'The chicken salad's your favourite as well as mine. And swapping out the dough sticks means we can have dessert.'

'Talking about food isn't going to get you out of telling me about Mr Hot. And I take it he's Mr rather than Dr, since he's a consultant?'

'Yes.' Joni blew out a breath. '*And* he's rostered on with me.'

Bailey gave her a wicked grin. 'Then I hope he's a better doctor than he is a dancer.'

Joni couldn't help smiling. 'He is. He's kind, he listens and he's got good patient skills.'

'But?'

She wriggled uncomfortably on her seat. 'I had a *fling* with him on Saturday night, Bailey. I went home with him and I spent the night with him. And he was a complete stranger!'

Bailey flapped a dismissive hand. 'It's not

as if you make a habit of it, Joni. It's the first time you've ever had a one-night stand in all the years I've known you. You're the poster child for "good girl", so lighten up and don't be so hard on yourself. Besides, Saturday was a tough day for you. I think you needed something to take your mind off it.' She looked her friend straight in the eye. 'So is he as hot in a white coat as he was in that shirt on Saturday?'

Joni felt the betraying colour seep into her skin.

Bailey grinned. 'Ah. Don't tell me he wears glasses.'

Joni could only nod. Busted. Big time. Bailey knew exactly what made up Joni's perfect man.

Bailey's grin broadened. 'And he looks as hot as Robert Downey Jr in said glasses?'

Joni put her face in her hands. 'I'm not answering that one.'

'You don't have to, sweetie.' Bailey reached over to squeeze her shoulder. 'This is good. You've met a guy who's actually nice—not like Marty the Maggot. Bonus, he's hot as well and he ticks all your boxes. I know he likes you, because of the way he was looking at you on the dance floor. And you've got stuff in common because of your job. Wins all round. So when are you going out on a date?'

'We're not.'

'Ah. The sticking point. Don't tell me—his pride's still hurting that you walked out on him without a word?'

Joni rolled her eyes. 'I didn't walk out on him without a word. I left him a note.'

'A short one,' Bailey agreed. 'So what's the problem, then?'

Joni grimaced. 'We're colleagues and it'd be way too awkward. He brought it up, actually. When we had lunch.'

Bailey blinked. 'You had lunch with him?'

'Because I was briefing him on the department, in between ward rounds and the TB clinic. Lunch was the only gap I had, so don't get ideas,' Joni said swiftly. 'Anyway, we agreed that today was the first time we met. Just so it's not awkward in the future.'

'Hmm.' Bailey turned to the waitress and thanked her for bringing their drinks and salads. 'OK, Joni, I get that you're both worried that things might be awkward at work. Fair point. But is there still chemistry between you?'

Joni sighed. 'He's out of my league, Bailey.'

'I've met him, so I'm qualified to argue with that statement,' Bailey pointed out. 'And I notice you didn't answer my question, which means the answer's yes.'

'It's one-sided.' Joni grimaced. 'And I'm never going to put myself in another situation where I'm the one who puts in most of the emotional effort.'

'Marty the Maggot,' Bailey said, 'has an awful lot to answer for.'

'Not just Marty,' Joni said ruefully. 'We both know how good I am at picking Mr Wrong. The one who starts off as a sweetie but ends up being more and more distant the longer we're together, or wants to change me once he really gets to know me.'

'And makes you feel that you're not good enough, so you apologise all the time when you really don't need to. But you've given that up now—or, at least, you're trying to,' Bailey said.

'Anyway, how do you know it's one-sided between you and Mr Hot?'

'I just do.'

'Hmm,' was all Bailey said. 'It didn't look one-sided on Saturday night.'

'Well, it is. He's made it very clear that he's not interested.'

'Maybe,' Bailey said thoughtfully, 'he dated the female version of Marty the Maggot. Someone who stomped all over his heart. Maybe you'd be good for each other.'

'We're colleagues, and that's all,' Joni said. 'And you're one to talk. When was the last time you dated?'

'Not long enough ago,' Bailey said, 'and we're not talking about me.'

Joni, remembering the way her best friend's life had imploded two years ago, reached over and squeezed her hand. 'Sorry—I didn't mean it like that. Just that maybe it's time you took your life off hold and let yourself meet someone and be happy again.'

'I appreciate the concern, but I'm perfectly fine as I am,' Bailey said, returning the pressure on her hand. 'Besides, this isn't about me. It's about you and Mr Hot.'

'Not going to happen,' Joni said. 'Now, shut up, or you get no pudding *and* I'll tell Jenna that you want to do extra warrior poses in the next class.'

'That's mean. OK. I'll shut up,' Bailey said.

'And no thinking either,' Joni warned.

Bailey gave her an innocent look that didn't have Joni fooled in the slightest.

It was just because he'd been celibate for months. Stupid physical feelings that he could tame in the gym, Aaron told himself.

Well, celibate except for Saturday night.

He couldn't even blame that one on alcohol, because half a glass of beer and a glass of champagne weren't enough to make him let down all his barriers. He'd been in full control of his actions.

He'd just been stupid and let desire out-talk his common sense when he'd seen Joni on the dance floor.

He added more weights to the bar, just so he'd

have to concentrate on what he was doing and wouldn't be able to think about emotional stuff. About sex. About Joni Parker.

She was his colleague. And, even if she weren't, there were a hundred other reasons why she should be off limits. He didn't want emotional stuff messing up his focus on his new job. He'd just been promoted to consultant. He didn't have time to be distracted.

But the weights weren't working. They weren't diverting his thoughts from her.

The rowing machine didn't help either.

And neither did the treadmill, even though he pushed himself to his limit.

Aaron's shirt was soaked by the time he'd finished his workout at the gym, but working his muscles to fatigue hadn't gone anywhere near making him too tired to think.

'She's off limits,' he told himself firmly. Out loud. In an attempt to make his head listen.

Except it wasn't working. Because he couldn't stop thinking about her. Wanting her. Wondering, *what if...?*

* * *

On Thursday, a teenage girl came in to the walk-in clinic with her stepmother and younger sister. Mrs Stone looked worried sick, but managed to give Joni a rundown that tallied with the notes their family doctor had sent. 'She's had a temperature for a couple of days but she feels cold all the time, she's been sick, and she's got a headache. None of the painkillers the doctor gave us has done anything to help it.' She bit her lip. 'I was worried it might be meningitis, but I couldn't see a rash. And the doctor said to come and see you because it might be Lyme disease.'

'Have you been staying in an area that's prone to ticks?' Joni asked.

The girl said nothing—clearly she was feeling too ill to talk—and Mrs Stone shrugged helplessly. 'I don't know, really. We went camping in Colorado. You know, hiking, that sort of thing. Our doctor thinks she might've been bitten by a tick.'

It was a possibility. 'I need to examine you, Josie,' Joni said gently to the girl. 'I know it's a bit embarrassing, but I'm going to have to ask you to take your clothes off. If I step outside the cubicle, can you take your clothes off for me?'

The girl nodded, and Joni stepped outside with Mrs Stone and the little girl, to give Josie some privacy.

'If she's been bitten and the tick was a carrier of Lyme disease, I'd expect to see a rash,' Joni said. 'How long ago were you there?'

'We've been back four days, and we went for a fortnight,' Mrs Stone said.

'OK. If the bite happened just before you came back, then the rash might not be visible yet and antibodies to the bacteria might not show up in the blood tests—we might have to do another blood test in a couple of weeks,' Joni warned. 'But you're in the right place. We'll find out what's wrong with her.'

She stepped back into the cubicle, followed by Mrs Stone and the little girl, and examined the girl gently. There was absolutely no sign of a rash. So it could be Lyme disease, or it could be something completely different. 'Does anything hurt, apart from your head?' she asked.

Josie shook her head very slightly.

'OK. You've definitely got an infection, but I'm going to need to do some blood tests to find out exactly what's causing the infection,' Joni said. 'In the meantime I'm going to start on you some broad-spectrum antibiotics to start dealing with the bugs that are making you ill. And I want to admit you to the ward, because I want to keep an eye on your temperature. It's up to you if you want to get dressed again, or if you'd rather I can get you a hospital gown to wear until your mum can bring you some pyjamas in.'

'She's not my mum,' Josie muttered, and Mrs Stone looked as if she'd been slapped.

Clearly there were family tensions here on top of what could turn out to be a serious illness, and that wasn't a good mix. Out of Josie's sight, Joni patted Mrs Stone's hand and mouthed, 'We'll talk in a minute.'

'OK, Josie. I'll leave you to get dressed,' she said to the teenager, 'and then I'm going to take some blood samples from you and send you for a chest X-ray.'

'Whatever,' Josie muttered.

'I'm sorry,' Mrs Stone said quietly when they'd

stepped away from the cubicle again. 'I'm her stepmother.' Her eyes filled with tears. 'She makes that very clear, even though her mum left years and years ago and hasn't bothered with her ever since. We used to get on, when I first married her dad, and it was even OK when I had Ruby, because we really tried to make Josie feel included and important as a big sister. But it hasn't been good for us as a family for a while.' She sighed. 'I guess because she's a teenager and she's trying to find out where she fits in the world. That's why we went on a family hiking trip. We thought it would give her a chance to chill out a bit, away from all the influences of social media, and maybe then she'd go back to being the sweet kid I first met.'

'Teenagers are hard and families are compli-cated.' Joni squeezed her hand. 'Don't blame yourself.'

'But if she got bitten by something that's made her sick, then it's my fault. I should've pulled rank and *made* her use the insect repellent spray instead of letting her get away with having a strop and refusing to do it.' Mrs Stone looked anguished. 'She said the smell made her feel sick and she wasn't going to use it. At the time, it just seemed like an extra battle I was going to lose and it wasn't worth the effort. I wish— I just *wish...*' Her words were cut off by a sob.

'Apart from the fact that you can't force a teenager to do something they really don't want to do, insect repellents aren't a hundred per cent effective in any case—so this *isn't* your fault,' Joni said. 'Right now I don't know what's causing the infection, but the chest X-ray and the blood tests might give me more of a clue. In the meantime, I'm going to give her some antibiotics—something broad-spectrum that will kill most bugs, and if the blood tests show that we can give her a better, more specific antibiotic, we'll switch over to that. Try not to worry.'

Later that afternoon, the test results showed that Josie's chest X-ray was clear, but her white blood cell count was slightly elevated. It would be another couple of days before the blood tests for Lyme disease came back, so it was a matter of being patient and hoping that the antibiotics would start to make a difference to the infection.

Joni was in the middle of seeing another patient when Nancy stepped into the cubicle. 'I'm really sorry to interrupt, Dr Parker. I need an urgent word.'

This didn't sound good. Joni apologised to her patient, and stepped into the corridor with Nancy. 'What is it?'

'Josie Stone. I think she's going into shock.'

Oh, no. Please don't let it be septic shock, Joni begged silently. With septic shock, chemicals released into the blood by the body's immune system to fight an infection triggered inflammation throughout the body. This led to blood clotting in the veins and arteries, which reduced the blood supply to the body's organs; once deprived of oxygen and nutrients, the organs could begin to fail.

Joni went straight to the ward and examined the girl swiftly. Josie's blood pressure was low, her temperature had spiked despite the medication Joni had given her, and although the girl was talking she sounded rambling and confused.

This wasn't looking good. All the symptoms pointed to septic shock, so they needed to act fast.

'Is Aaron around?' she asked Nancy quietly.

'I'll get him,' she said.

Josie was already on antibiotics; Joni quickly put her on intravenous fluids to deal with any potential blood-clotting problem and keep her blood pressure stable. 'I'm going to put a mask on you now, Josie,' she said, 'with oxygen, to help you breathe more easily, OK?'

Aaron came on to the ward. 'Nancy said you needed me.'

And his cool, calm demeanour was just what she needed to stem the panic rising through her. She filled him in on Josie's case history and the treatment regime she'd started.

'That's everything I would've done,' he said.

Meaning that the treatment would work? Because she had a bad, bad feeling about this. Nothing she could put her finger on, but something wasn't right. Josie had had a second dose of antibiotics and they should be starting to work by now. Her symptoms shouldn't be getting worse.

As if Aaron could read her mind, he said, 'We can run a couple more blood tests, but all we can do now really is wait for the antibiotics to work on that infection, and wait for the other test results to come back. Hang on in there.' He touched her shoulder briefly in a gesture of solidarity. 'And call me if you need me, OK?'

Joni took more blood samples; as she left Josie's bedside, she noticed that little Ruby was sobbing quietly next to her mother. Poor kid. She was clearly worried sick. Joni took a tissue out of her pocket, crouched down to Ruby's level and handed her the tissue. 'Here you go,' she said softly.

Ruby rubbed it across her nose. 'Thank you,' she said between tears.

'I know this is scary, but don't worry,' Joni said. 'We're doing our best to make your big sister better. She's in the right place and we're looking after her.'

'But it's my fault she's sick,' Ruby sobbed.

'It's not your fault, sweetie. Sometimes these things just happen,' Joni reassured her.

'But it *is* my fault. I wished she'd get sick, and

she did.' She gulped. 'Josie's always so mean to me. And I wanted her to be sick so then she'd be sorry about the squirrel.'

A memory stirred in the back of Joni's head about an article she'd read recently about Colorado and diseases in rodents. 'What happened with the squirrel?' she asked gently.

'It died. I wanted to bury it, but Mummy said I couldn't and I had to leave it. I sneaked back because I knew if you didn't bury the squirrel then it wouldn't get to heaven. I made a cross and a flower crown for it. I was going to bury it and say a prayer, but Josie followed me and she picked it up and threw it down the ravine. Stuff came out of the squirrel and went all over her— it was horrible!' Her face grew anguished. 'And she said—' Her breath hitched. 'Josie said if I told anyone about it I'd be in real trouble.'

Joni squeezed Ruby's hand reassuringly. 'You're not in trouble, sweetie, not at all. Actually, you might have told me something that will help her get better. Can you tell me when this happened?'

'It was the last day of our holiday. That's why

Mummy said she didn't want me to bury the squirrel, because there wasn't enough time and I was supposed to go and pack my stuff.'

'That's really helpful, Ruby,' Joni said softly. 'Thank you. I'll be back really soon to see you all, but I need to get these blood samples off for testing and check out a few other things.'

The little girl gave her a watery smile. 'Is Josie going to be all right?'

Until they knew for sure what was wrong, that wasn't a promise Joni wanted to make. 'I'll try my very best to make her better. And she's in absolutely the right place.'

CHAPTER FIVE

JONI WENT BACK to her office and checked the computer swiftly for the article she remembered seeing, printed it out, and went to find Aaron.

'I'm pretty sure Josie Stone doesn't have Lyme disease,' she said. She told him what Ruby had confided to her about the squirrel. 'I read an article a couple of months ago about rodents in Colorado and the bubonic plague.'

'And you really think it's that?' He looked sceptical. 'I don't want to burst your bubble, but I've never come across a case of plague yet, not in all the years I've worked in tropical medicine.'

'Neither have I, but look at this.' She showed him the printout. 'This is all about a teenager with sudden, severe septic shock in the chest, and the diagnosis turned out to be bubonic plague.'

He frowned. 'But aren't plague bacteria spread through flea bites?'

'Josie picked up the squirrel. If there were any fleas on the carcass, they could've bitten her—and it only takes one infected flea for the bacteria to spread,' Joni pointed out. 'I was looking for the bull's-eye rash of Lyme disease somewhere around her wrists and ankles, but there wasn't a rash of any kind when I examined her.'

'What about buboes?'

'None. No swelling at all on her lymph nodes in her armpits, and she said she didn't have any pain anywhere except her head. But, apart from the fact that plague doesn't always present with buboes,' she reminded him, 'the thing with the squirrel happened on the last day of their holiday. They've been back for four days, and the incubation period for plague is two to six days. She's been ill for a couple of days. It all fits, Aaron.'

'You've started her on a broad-spectrum antibiotic, yes?'

'But it might not be the right one.' She bit her lip. 'There's a very good chance it might already have moved from bubonic to septicaemic plague. We need more blood tests. And I think we need to give the whole family prophylactic antibiotics.'

'Good call,' he said, looking grim. 'Just as well Ruby told you.'

'Apart from the fact that she's blaming herself, poor kid.'

Aaron knew how that felt. He'd been a couple of years older than little Ruby when Ned had died, but he could remember it as clearly as if it had been yesterday. Knowing that his older brother's death was his fault. Knowing that the rest of the family blamed him, too—because if Ned hadn't thrown himself over Aaron to protect him from the blast, he wouldn't have been injured and gone to hospital. And if Ned hadn't gone to hospital, he wouldn't have caught malaria. And if he hadn't caught malaria and developed complications, he wouldn't have died. The chain of blame dragged on and on and on.

Even though part of Aaron knew that he'd been a child at the time and of course it hadn't all been his fault, he still couldn't rid himself of the guilt. He'd made it through the fallout from the bomb with a couple of tiny scratches and a bit of claustrophobia. Ned—who'd had so much to give the world—hadn't made it at all.

He shook himself. *Not now.* 'OK. Let's go and examine her.'

When Joni and Aaron examined Josie again, they discovered a couple of tiny bites on her arms, so tiny that they would've been easy to miss during the first examination. Aaron agreed that they looked like flea bites. There was still no sign of any swelling in the girl's lymph glands, but Joni was sure that it was plague.

'I think you're right. The infection's already moved from Josie's lymph nodes to her blood vessels,' Aaron said quietly. 'I agree. We need to get the lab to add an extra test into the blood they already have. For now we'll start her on different antibiotics and put her in isolation—and I want all nursing staff to be gowned and masked when they come in to her room to treat her.'

'OK. I'll let the public health department know, too,' Joni said. The plague—incredibly rare as it was—was a notifiable disease. 'And we'll keep an eye out for any sign of a rash. If she goes into DIC…'

Disseminated intravascular coagulation caused tiny blood clots to form throughout the body and depleted the blood's clotting resources, so the body could no longer control bleeding. One of the classic signs was a dark purple rash. And if Josie went into DIC and they couldn't get her blood clotting back under control, the girl wouldn't make it.

Aaron rested his hand briefly on Joni's shoulder. 'Hey. You spotted what it was, and we'll keep her under very close observation.'

'Uh-huh.' But Joni had a bad, bad feeling about this. The teenager wasn't out of the woods, not by a very long way. The later that treatment started, the less likely it was that the outcome would be good. Even with treatment, if it had already turned to septicaemic plague then there was a fifty-fifty chance that Josie wouldn't make it.

When Josie's stepmother came in to visit, Joni took her to one side for a quiet word first.

'There isn't an easy way to say this, Mrs Stone,' she said, 'so I'll go for the straight option, and I'm happy to answer any questions you might have. We're waiting on test results, but we're pretty sure we know what the infection is now. Josie has the plague.'

'The *plague*?' Mrs Stone looked shocked. 'What, you mean, like the thing that killed loads of people just before the Great Fire of London?'

'Yes.'

Mrs Stone shook her head as if trying to clear it. 'But I thought—I thought that had all died out years and years ago.'

'No. The plague's still around in some parts of the world,' Josie said. 'We need to give your whole family antibiotics, just in case Josie has passed the infection to any of you.'

Mrs Stone looked perplexed. 'But she didn't say she'd been bitten by anything, and I thought the plague was spread by rats?'

'It's actually spread by the fleas on the rats,' Joni said. 'Ruby told me something in confidence, and that's what made me connect Josie's condition with the plague.' She paused. 'I promised Ruby she wouldn't get into trouble.'

'Of course she won't get into trouble. What did she say?'

Joni explained what the little girl had told her about the squirrel and what Josie had done.

Mrs Stone looked horrified. 'Oh, my God. So both my girls could be infected?'

'I don't think Ruby actually touched the squirrel, and she isn't showing any of the symptoms that Josie has, so it's very unlikely that she was bitten by one of the fleas,' Joni said. She took Mrs Stone's hands. 'But I won't lie to you. It's not going to be an easy road ahead.'

'Could Josie d—?' Mrs Stone bit off the word, shuddered and stared at Joni in dismay. 'No. No. She can't. She just *can't*.'

'We're doing our best,' Joni told her. 'But she is very sick right now.'

Josie didn't seem to respond to the new antibiotic treatment, and the next morning Joni was in the middle of a clinic when Nancy sent Shelley, one of the newly qualified nurses, to fetch her. 'Josie Stone's arrested,' Shelley said. 'Mikey's there, but Nancy needs you, too.'

'I'll go straight there. Can you let Aaron know, please, Shelley, and ask Reception to explain to my patients that I've been called to an emergency so there will be a delay, and ask them to sort out cover for me? And then if you can ring Mrs Stone and ask her to come straight in, I'd really appreciate it,' Joni said.

'Yes, of course.'

'Thanks, Shelley.' Joni pulled on gloves, a gown and a mask as she headed to the isolation room, where Mikey and Nancy had already intubated the girl and were alternately doing chest compressions and ventilating her with the bag and mask.

The defibrillator was already charging. Joni applied the gel pads to Josie's chest. 'OK. Clear and ready to shock at two hundred,' she said, checking that everyone had taken their hands off the patient before she pressed down with the paddles to make sure Josie didn't arch off the bed, and delivered the first shock.

'No change,' Nancy called, looking at the monitor.

'OK. Charging to two hundred again. And clear!'

The second shock did nothing either. Hell, hell, hell. This *had* to work.

'Charging to three-sixty,' Joni said. 'And clear!'
Again, nothing.

'Administering adrenaline,' she said, taking the ampoule from Shelley, who'd come in to say that she'd left a message on Mrs Stone's answering machine and her voicemail, asking her to contact the hospital straight away. 'Mikey, are you still OK to do compressions?'

'I think we should switch over again—Mikey, take over the bagging,' Nancy said, and took over doing the compressions.

After a minute of CPR, there was still no change.

Joni changed the gel pads. 'OK. Round two. Charging to three-sixty. And clear!'

Still no response.

Aaron strode in to the room. 'Shelley got me up to speed. What do you need me to do?'

'Help with the CPR protocol. We're *not* going to lose her,' Joni said, and kept going with the defibrillator.

They kept checking the monitor for output after every shock, and they worked on Joni as a team for the next half an hour—all to no avail.

Finally Aaron put his hand on Joni's shoulder. 'She's gone, Joni. Do you want to call it, or do you want me to do it?'

Joni took in a gulp of air. 'One more round. Please. Just one more round.'

'She's gone,' he said gently. 'It's been half an hour. You know as well as I do it's not going to work now. Her heart stopped and, although we've been breathing for her and doing chest compressions, there will have been too much damage.'

Joni squeezed her eyes tightly shut to keep the tears back. Losing a patient was always hard—and it was rare in her department, so she'd never become even slightly accustomed to it happening. 'OK.' She took a deep breath and looked at the team. 'Does everyone else agree that I should call it?'

Mikey, Shelley and Nancy all gave her grim-faced nods.

'Time of death ten forty-five,' she said. 'Thanks for your efforts, everyone. It's…' She gulped hard, unable to continue. What could you say when a teenage girl had died? All that promise, all that bright future wiped out. How would her family ever get over it?

'We all did what we could,' Aaron said gently.

But it hadn't been enough. 'Are the Stones here yet?' Joni asked.

'I don't think so, or someone would've come in to tell us,' Nancy said.

Joni bit her lip. 'OK. I'll try calling Mrs Stone again.'

Except there was still no answer. This wasn't the kind of news Joni wanted to break remotely, so she simply left a message.

'Do you want me to tell them when they get here?' Aaron asked.

She shook her head. 'Josie is—*was*—my patient. And you've got people waiting in clinic.' As had she.

He gave her a searching look. 'Call me if you need me, OK?'

'Thanks.' She kept her words to a minimum, not trusting herself not to break down into tears. She wasn't going to be that unprofessional in front of him. 'Shelley, can you keep an eye out for the Stones and put them in the side room for me when they arrive, please?'

'Of course.' Shelley gave her a hug. 'Hang on in there, kiddo.'

Considering that she was actually a few years older than the nurse, the irony made Joni smile. 'You, too. And thanks.'

She'd just finished getting Josie ready for her family to see her and written up the paperwork when Shelley came in. 'They're here.' Her eyes were full of sympathy. 'Mrs Stone and the little girl.'

Oh, help. It was bad enough having to tell adults this kind of news. Telling a child that they'd just lost someone close...that was going to be really hard.

Joni took a deep breath and walked to the side room.

'How is she?' Mrs Stone stood up, looking anxious. 'When the nurse asked us to wait in here... She's worse, isn't she?'

Joni took her hand. 'I'm so sorry.' This was the bit of her job she really, really hated. It didn't happen very often, but she hated punching an unfillable hole in people's lives.

'She—she's not…?' Shock filled Mrs Stone's face.

'Her heart stopped working this morning,' Joni said gently. 'We did everything we could to get her heart started again, but she was just too sick. I'm so sorry.'

Both Mrs Stone and Ruby were devastated by the news; Joni spent the next few minutes comforting them, feeling utterly helpless and wishing that she'd found a way to save Josie.

Later that afternoon, Aaron walked in to the office where Joni was writing up her notes from the afternoon clinic. He could see that she'd been crying, because her eyes were still red and slightly puffy. And he knew exactly what had upset her.

'Are you OK?' he asked gently.

She bit her lip. 'Not really. We don't lose many patients here and it always hits me for six. Especially when it's a child. I…' She gulped. 'That's why I could never work in the emergency department. I don't think I'd be able to cope with losing patients in those kinds of numbers.'

'It wasn't your fault. You followed all the right protocols and you put all the pieces together to see what we'd all missed,' Aaron said.

'And it still wasn't enough.' She lifted her chin. 'I'm sorry. I shouldn't be burdening you with this. Anyway, I rang my mum and I'm going home when I've finished my paperwork. I'll be better after an evening of TLC with my family.'

TLC.

From your family.

Aaron stood there, feeling awkward. He knew he should at least offer her a hug—it was what you'd do to comfort a colleague—but he could still remember what it felt like to hold Joni close, and he didn't trust himself not to do something stupid. Like trying to kiss away her sadness. And, at the same time, part of him felt wistful and a tiny bit envious. How good it must be to have a family that supportive—to know that when you'd had a bad day you could call and they'd make everything better, and they wouldn't despise you for showing the least sign of weakness.

His own family was much more distant—and not just geographically. Ever since Ned's death… He pushed the thought away. *Not now.* He wasn't going to let all the misery seep through him now. 'Well, if there's anything I can do,' he said, hoping that she wasn't actually going to take him up on the offer because he hated dealing with emotional stuff, 'you know where I am.'

She nodded. 'Yes. And thank you.'

'No problem.'

'Aaron, are you OK?' she asked, shocking him. Nobody ever asked him how he felt.

'I'm fine,' he said.

'Josie was your patient, too, so you must be feeling as bad as I am. Why don't you come to my parents' place with me after you finish your shift?' she asked.

He was tempted.

But that would be a huge step towards getting involved with her. Involvement led to pain and misery. So keeping his distance would be the sensible way of dealing with it. 'Thanks for the offer,' he said, 'but I'm fine. I'll probably go and take it out in the gym.'

'My friend Bailey would approve of that. Endorphins are good,' she said with an attempt at a smile.

'They certainly are.' He forced himself to smile back. 'See you later.'

The department felt subdued for the following week. Even the beginning of the departmental evening out on the following Saturday night was quiet, until the demands of the climbing wall made everyone concentrate on the physical movements instead of the ache in their hearts.

It was the first time that Joni had seen Aaron wearing jeans. It made him look younger and less remote. And she loved the T-shirt he was wearing—a *pi* sign with six extra 'legs' and the word 'octopi' written above it. It was the kind of geek joke she'd always enjoyed.

'He hasn't mentioned a partner to me,' Nancy said softly.

'Who hasn't?' Josie asked.

Nancy rolled her eyes. 'Love, I could see you

watching him just now. You know exactly who I mean. Why don't you ask him out?'

Because he'd already made it clear that he didn't want to repeat what had happened between them at the salsa club. Not that Joni wanted any of her colleagues to know about that night. It made her feel too ashamed. She fell back on a safe excuse. 'Because we work together. It'll make things too embarrassing and awkward at work when he turns me down.'

'Sweetie, what makes you think he'd turn you down?' Nancy asked.

Joni grimaced. Wasn't it obvious?

'I could strangle that Marty—except I wouldn't be first in the queue,' Nancy said. 'He was never good enough for you and he knew it—that's why he did a hatchet job on your self-esteem. Ending your engagement was the best thing you ever did. And you really need to take that extra step and start seeing someone else, to let you finish getting over him.'

Joni gave her a wry smile. 'You've been talking to Bailey.'

'No, love, I'm just saying what everyone

thinks. You're a lovely girl and you have so much to give, and…' Nancy smiled at her. 'And I bet your mum's already said all that to you, hasn't she?'

'Well, yes,' Joni admitted. 'And so have my brothers, and my dad, and my grandmothers…'

'There you are, then.'

'It's not going to happen, Nancy. It's best to be just colleagues.' And Joni spent the rest of the evening trying not to think about that other Saturday night. Because she knew she'd be a fool to think that it could happen again.

CHAPTER SIX

THE FOLLOWING WEEK, the day of the team-building exercises arrived. Joni, Aaron and the new F1 doctor Mikey were sent to the outdoor adventure centre, together with medical staff from the emergency department, the children's ward and the maternity department.

After a briefing meeting, the course leader sent them on an outdoor obstacle course where they had to work as a team. At each obstacle one team member had to trust the others to lift them over the obstacle or guide them blindfold through part of the course.

'Third place. That isn't bad,' Aaron said as their team reached the finish line.

'You worked well together,' the course leader said with a smile. 'It's a great start.'

And, oh, please let it all be over soon, so we

can get back to the hospital and look after our patients again, Joni thought.

'The next challenge,' the course leader said after they'd had a short break for tea and biscuits, 'is a treasure hunt, in pairs. We'll give each pair a map and the first clue, which will lead to you the next clue, and so on. The final clue will lead you to a box with a message inside. The first pair to call us with the message is the winner, and we'll brief you on the next activity over lunch.'

And they'd get a chance to dry out a bit, Joni hoped. It had rained for the last five days solid, so the obstacle course had left them all covered in mud.

'And the pairs are...'

She waited while the course leader divided everyone into groups. Maybe this time the leader would mix up the different departments so they were working as part of a bigger team instead of a group within their own wards.

Then, halfway through, she heard him say, 'Joni Parker and Aaron Hughes.'

Oh, great. Aaron had been quiet enough so

far today. And she'd made it worse by blushing when he'd lifted her up during the first activity, remembering how he'd carried her to his bed that night after the salsa club. She'd caught his eye and the heat in his expression had told her that he was remembering, too—which was a complication they could both do without.

'So. You and me,' Aaron said, his voice neutral.

Was he embarrassed, disappointed—wary, even? She didn't have a clue. Normally, Joni was reasonably good at reading people, but she found Aaron a puzzle. 'Uh-huh.' She looked at the map and the clue; pretending to study them was a lot easier than facing Aaron. 'I think we should be heading here.' She pointed at location on the map.

He read the clue and nodded. 'Agreed.'

It didn't take them long to reach their first location and discover their next clue. It was an easy anagram, and they both said the word at the same time.

'Teamwork,' Aaron said softly. 'We think along the same lines.'

Maybe in a work situation, Joni thought, but definitely not on a personal level. Although Aaron was perfectly friendly and polite to everyone in the department, she could sense that he was keeping just a little bit of distance between himself and everyone else. He fitted in very well, on the surface; but he didn't really connect with anyone on a deeper level. He kept himself in reserve.

Which made her wonder even more why he'd asked her back to his flat the night they'd met at the salsa club. It just wasn't Aaron-like behaviour.

Not that she could ask him. That was way, way too personal. She'd learned over the last couple of weeks that Aaron didn't do personal. He was a good doctor, brilliant with patients, and he worked incredibly hard—even staying on past the end of his shift to coach some of the younger members of the team—but she still knew practically no more about him than she had on the day they'd first met.

He deflected any personal question, usually by smiling and asking the other person about something so they were distracted away from the subject. Which intrigued her—what was he hiding?—but at the same time it made her wary of him. Emotional distance was what had wrecked all her past relationships. She'd be crazy to get involved with yet another man who was emotionally distant. Yet still something about him drew her. Who was the man behind the barriers? She'd glimpsed him a couple of times and she'd liked what she'd seen.

She shook herself. Tough? This was meant to be a professional team-building day, not a time to start fantasising about a man who'd already made it clear that their fling had been just that. A one-off. Finished.

The final clue took them to a tunnel at the edge of the woodland.

'You take the left hand of the tunnel and I'll take the right, and whoever finds the clue calls the other?' Aaron asked.

'Fine by me,' she said, and switched on her torch to help her see in the gloom.

Joni had just found the box containing their

message when there was a roar and a crash, and the dim light in the tunnel went out completely.

'Aaron, are you all right?' she called.

'Yes. I'm over here.'

She saw a patch of light shining on the floor, showing her where he was in the tunnel.

'Are you OK?' he asked.

'Yes. What just happened?' she asked.

'Given that it's been so wet this month, I'd guess part of the roof got over-saturated and fell in,' he said.

'And it's blocked our exit—that's why it just got darker?'

'That's the most likely answer,' he said.

'OK. I'm coming over to you and then we can check it out together.' She shoved the small box in her pocket, then picked her way over to him carefully, keeping the beam of her torch on the floor so she could see where she was walking and stopping every so often to check that she was still heading towards him; in the complete darkness it was easy to get disorientated.

Together, they made their way carefully to where the entrance of the tunnel had been and shone their torches around. All Joni could see was a pile of rubble. 'Maybe we can dig ourselves out,' she suggested.

He bent to take a closer look and rubbed some of the soil between his fingers. 'Better not. It's sandstone and the roof needs stabilising. If we try tunnelling out, we could trigger another roof fall and end up getting buried in the middle of it.'

'That sounds as if you're talking from experience,' she said.

'You could say that.' His voice was dry.

'I'll ring back to base and let them know what's happened.' She took her mobile phone from her pocket. 'Oh, great—no signal.' She rolled her eyes.

'Probably because we're underground,' he said.

She knew what he meant. 'My phone's like that sometimes in the middle of a shopping precinct—it just can't pick up a signal. So we're not even going to be able to send a text to tell anyone that we're stuck here.'

'I'll try my phone, just in case I can get a signal.' There was a pause, then a sigh. 'No. It's the same with mine.'

'So what do we do? Take turns trying to dig ourselves out—but being *really* careful?'

'Apart from the fact we don't have anything we can use as a shovel to move the earth, it's really not safe to try digging out,' he said. 'Not with a fragile rock like sandstone.'

Just to back him up, there was another rumble and more earth fell from the ceiling.

'I guess if the organisers haven't heard from us by lunchtime, they'll realise something's wrong. If they try to call us they'll guess that we don't have a signal, and then they'll start looking for us and get us out of here safely,' he said. 'Right now we need to find a safe spot where the roof isn't likely to collapse on us, and we'll just have to wait it out until they come to find us.'

'Right,' she said. Great. Trapped in a tunnel with a man who wasn't keen on small talk—and who seemed to avoid deeper, personal stuff as much as he could. The time was going to go very slowly indeed.

He sounded concerned as he asked, 'Are you OK insulin-wise?'

'I'm fine,' she said, though she appreciated

the fact that he'd actually asked. 'I take it twice a day so I'm not actually due to take it again until this evening. Though I always have a supply with me as well as fast-acting carbs, so I can deal with a blood sugar problem either way.' She paused. 'How do we know if there's a safe spot to wait? Or could the whole roof fall in on us?' Even the idea of it made her feel suddenly nervous.

'We listen to find out if we can hear anything, then shine our torches round to see if there are any other areas where rubble's fallen,' he said. 'Oh, and keep the beam on the ground. In this environment, it'll hurt if a torch shines in your eyes because your pupils are at maximum dilation.'

They were both silent. Joni could hear nothing; and when she shone her torch around she couldn't see any new-looking piles of rubble or earth. Hopefully that meant the rest of the roof of the tunnel was stable.

'I think we'll be safe over here,' Aaron said, and found them a spot near the wall. 'But we'd better not sit directly on the ground or we'll lose too much body heat.' He took off his jacket and spread it on the ground. 'Let's sit on this. My jacket's waterproof, so we won't get wet.'

'Aren't you going to be cold without a jacket?' she asked.

He shrugged. 'I'll be fine.'

'How do you know all this stuff?' she asked. 'Did you used to do rock-climbing or something?'

'Manchester's very near the Peak District. Some of the people I knew in the emergency department were in the local mountain rescue team, working with climbers and cavers,' he explained.

He'd said 'people I knew', not 'friends', she noted. 'And you were part of that, too?' she asked.

'Not me,' he said. 'Caving's never been my thing.'

'That sounded a bit heartfelt,' she said.

'I guess.' Though she noticed that he didn't offer any further information, and she didn't push him. It felt too intrusive to ask anything more.

And then he surprised her by filling the

silence. 'I got buried in rubble when I was about eight. So I don't tend to do underground stuff by choice,' he said.

'That's understandable. What happened?' Then she caught herself. 'Sorry. I'm being nosey.'

'Strike one for your sorry jar,' he said. 'I pretty much invited the question.'

She wasn't sure whether to be more shocked that he'd remembered she was trying to break her apology habit, or that he was actually volunteering information about himself. And her silence lasted long enough for him to fill it again.

'Bomb,' he said economically. 'My parents were in the armed forces. We were in a war zone at the time. I was at home after school when our house was hit.'

'Did it take the rescue party long to get you out?' she asked.

'It felt like hours,' he said. 'It probably wasn't anywhere near that long, but when you're young and scared and in the dark under a pile of rubble, you tend to lose all sense of time.' His voice went decidedly neutral, as if he was picking his words carefully and taking out all the emotional stuff.

'My parents sent me back to boarding school in England so I'd be safe, well away from the war zone.'

Safe but lonely, she thought, sent away from his family; no doubt he'd felt as if he'd been punished for being scared. Even though people much older and more experienced in life than an eight-year-old boy would be terrified and have nightmares about it if they'd been caught under a pile of rubble after an explosion. For a young child, it must have been an incredibly scary experience. 'That must've been hard on you,' she said softly.

He shrugged again. 'I survived. What about you? Have you ever gone caving?'

She laughed. 'No, that's way too dangerous for me. I'm afraid I'm a bit of a wuss. I've spent most of my life wrapped in cotton wool.'

'Because you're diabetic?'

'Partly.' She wrinkled her nose. 'It's a long story. I guess, like you said, we just have to sit tight and wait it out.'

He nodded. 'I don't know how long we're

going to be here, so we ought to conserve our light. Are you OK with being in the dark if we switch the torches off?'

She had a feeling that he might not be, after his experiences as a child. And that he'd never admit it. If she took his hand to offer him comfort, she was pretty sure he'd pull away. Whereas if he thought he was giving *her* comfort and strength, maybe he'd feel less awkward about it. 'I don't mind the dark, so much,' she said. 'But don't let me think about spiders, OK?'

He switched off the light. 'Spiders are far more scared of you than you are of them, you know.'

'I wouldn't bet on that.' She guessed that he might not want the headspace to remember how it felt to be buried in rubble, alone and in the dark. 'Talk to me about something else to take my mind off the spiders,' she invited.

'Like what?'

She knew it was a personal question and he'd probably deflect it, but she asked anyway. 'What made you decide to specialise in tropical medicine and infectious diseases?'

* * *

Of all the things she could have asked. Aaron groaned inwardly.

Maybe he should make something up. Say he'd had a mad crush on the tropical medicine lecturer at university, something like that. But the words just wouldn't come. The silence stretched longer and longer and longer, and he still couldn't think of a decent reason. Finally, he mumbled the truth. 'My brother had malaria.'

'So you wanted to work in the specialty that saved him—like a kind of payback?' she asked.

Far, far worse than that. And it felt as if he was choking as the words forced their way out. 'It didn't save him.'

He heard her shocked gasp. Soft. Guilty.

Though no amount of guilt could ever match the amount that had built up on his soul over the years.

He felt her hand fumbling for his, squeezing his fingers. 'I'm sorry. That must have been so hard for you. For all your family.'

Yeah. His parents had never been the same, after. Third-generation armed forces, they'd always had a fairly stiff upper lip—but after Ned's death it had been permafrosted as well. And they'd sent him away. So he'd be safe—but he knew that it had also been so his presence wouldn't remind them of what they'd lost.

'It was my fault.'

Oh, hell. He hadn't meant to tell her that. But the words had slippcd out when he wasn't paying attention.

Her fingers were still wrapped round his. How? How could she bear to be anywhere near him, now she knew the ugly truth about him?

'What happened?' she asked, her voice gentle. So sweet. So soft.

His first instinct was to pull away. His second was to hold her close and take comfort from her. Torn between the two, he was frozen.

'Aaron?'

She clearly wasn't going to let this go. She wasn't letting his hand go either. Hating himself, but not seeing any other option—because they were stuck here together alone in the dark and he had no idea how long it would be until they were rescued—he gave in. 'The bomb... I wasn't on my own in the house. My brother had come home early from sixth form. I was hungry, and he was making me a sandwich.' Easygoing, sweet-tempered Ned—the one person in the family who hadn't minded Aaron trailing along behind him or seen him as a nuisance. Aaron had always known he was an accidental baby—eight years younger than Ned, ten years younger than his sister, twelve years younger than his oldest brother. With an age gap like that, of course he hadn't been planned. But Ned hadn't made him feel like an unwanted nuisance. He'd built model planes with Aaron, taught him to play cricket. Aaron had adored him.

And his death weighed so heavily on Aaron's shoulders. Even now, nearly a quarter of a century later, the guilt hadn't lessened one bit.

'When the first blast hit, he threw me to the floor and covered me, to keep me safe. Except he was injured by the rubble. I couldn't do anything to help him—just talk to him and tell him stupid jokes, anything to make the time pass until someone came to dig us out.' He dragged in a breath. Why the hell was he telling Joni all this? He never spoke about Ned. Never.

But being trapped in a tunnel with falling rubble had brought it all back so clearly that he couldn't stop the words tumbling out.

'They dug us out eventually. Took Ned to hospital. But someone slipped up with the malaria tablets. You know how it happens. Even if you take the tablets all the time, they're not a hundred per cent protection. And if you miss a couple and you get bitten by a mosquito...' He closed his eyes, but he could still see Ned's face. 'He caught malaria.'

'*Falciparum?*' she asked.

The most serious type of malaria. The one that caused complications. The fatal kind.

'Yes.' The word was ripped from him.

'I'm sorry. That must've been hard on you.'

Particularly as he'd hardly ever been allowed to visit Ned. It had been made very clear to Aaron that he mustn't be a nuisance—the baby of the family who always got in the way. He gave a soft huff of agreement.

'But, Aaron—you were only eight when it happened. A child. It wasn't your fault.'

Could she really not see it? The chain of causality was so simple. 'If Ned hadn't thrown himself over me, he wouldn't have been injured by the rubble, so he wouldn't have gone to hospital, and then he wouldn't have caught malaria.'

'I have two younger brothers,' she said. 'And if you were eight when your brother was in sixth form, then there's pretty much the same gap between us as there was between you and Ned. I'm six years older than Olly, and eight years older than Luke. And I can assure you that if we'd been in those circumstances, I would've done exactly the same as Ned did.'

It didn't help. At all.

'If I'd been hurt in the rubble, I wouldn't have blamed my brothers,' she added softly. 'They weren't the ones who launched the bombs.'

Intellectually, Aaron knew that Joni was speaking the truth. But, in his heart, he'd never forgive himself for Ned's loss. Never forgive himself for being the one who'd survived.

As if she'd read his thoughts, she said, 'I know

I'm speaking out of turn, but it sounds to me as if you've got survivor guilt.'

He didn't answer.

'And I bet your parents blame themselves just as much,' she said. 'Because they weren't there when it happened.'

'That's ridiculous. It wasn't their fault.'

'And it definitely wasn't yours.'

He wasn't going to bother arguing that one with her. 'Ned had so much to give. He was going to be a doctor. And he would've been a really good one.'

'Is that why you became a doctor? Because he didn't have the chance and you wanted to make up for that?' she asked.

'Partly,' Aaron admitted. 'And I guess part of me wanted to be like him. But I'm a doctor for me, too. So I can help people.' Save them. Make a difference. And not feel as helpless as he had during Ned's final decline.

'Did anyone give you counselling after he died?'

'No.' A family who believed in stiff upper lips most definitely didn't believe in counselling.

You never, ever talked to people about things. You just got on with it and ignored how you were feeling. And he really shouldn't be talking to her about this now.

'Maybe it's worth talking to someone,' she suggested. 'Someone who can help you to see for yourself that it really wasn't your fault.'

'I know it wasn't, and I'm fine,' he lied. He needed to get her off the subject. Now. And there was only one way he could think of to do it, even though it felt like scraping the scabs off his own wounds. 'Tell me about your brothers.'

It was the first time Aaron had asked her anything really personal, Joni thought. And she was just beginning to understand what made him tick. The youngest child of an armed forces family, having to go wherever they were posted and never really having the chance to settle and make friends. In some ways, she thought, that would tend to draw a family closer together, because they'd be the only constant thing in each other's life. Or maybe instead they'd had to grow hard shells and not let themselves get too attached to anyone, including each other. Especially given his older brother's death. It explained why Aaron was always polite and fitted in with everyone, but at the same time he kept that bit of distance between himself and other people. Because he was scared of getting close to someone and then risk losing them, the way he'd lost his brother.

'Luke's a trainee architect and Olly's a music teacher—by day, anyway,' she said. 'By night and at weekends, he's the lead guitarist in a rock band.'

'You sound proud of him,' Aaron said.

'I am. He's brilliant and I always go to see him play when he has a gig. So does Luke—they both live in London. And we often get to have dinner together first and catch up on everything. I love both my brothers to bits.' She laughed. 'Even if they do boss me about.'

'But you're the oldest—shouldn't you be the bossy one?' he asked, sounding surprised.

She laughed again. 'I've tried telling them that, but they don't listen to a word of it. I guess they're a bit overprotective because of the dia-betes.'

'Lots of people live with diabetes,' Aaron said. 'It sounds as if there's more of a story to it than that.'

'I guess the way we found out about it was a bit dramatic,' she said. 'We didn't actually know I was diabetic. Then I went round Europe with Bailey in the summer holidays at the end of our first year as medical students. You know, that thing where your ticket means you can travel on any train throughout Europe for a whole month. We tried to explore as many places as we could. I hadn't been feeling brilliant, but no way was I going to spoil our trip by moaning about feeling ill. We'd just travelled from Rome to Venice, and that's where I collapsed. I ended up being rushed to hospital on a water ambulance. Not that I re-member any of it.' She shrugged. 'It turned out that I had DKA, so I was kept in for a couple of days.'

Joni had spoken lightly, but Aaron knew as well as she did that diabetic ketoacidosis could have been fatal. A collapse like that meant hospital treatment; the medics would've needed to resuscitate her, clear the ketones from her blood, correct her electrolyte imbalance and then start insulin treatment to stabilise her. No wonder her family had gone super-protective. They must've been terrified that they'd lose her. 'You'd really had no idea that you might be diabetic?'

'None at all. I'd been feeling tired and a bit sick for a few days, but I assumed that was because we were doing a lot of walking in the midday sun. I'd lost my hat a couple of days before, and hadn't quite got round to replacing it—I thought maybe I had slight sunstroke, and that was why I was thirsty all the time and needed to drink a lot.'

The symptoms were similar to those of undiagnosed diabetes, he knew, so it had been a fair call. Especially to a first-year medical student. 'It must've been pretty scary for your friend, being in the middle of a medical emergency in a foreign country.'

'Luckily for us, Bailey's mum is Italian, so Bailey can speak the language really well. She was able to translate for me when the doctors came round, and also for Mum and Dad,' Joni explained. 'They came rushing straight out to Venice when Bailey rang them from the hospital. 'So that's mostly why my family's a bit overprotective.' He could hear the wry smile in Joni's voice as she added, 'I never did get to have that gondola ride Bailey and I were planning.'

'Maybe one day,' he said. 'So you've travelled a lot?'

'Not really. When I was young, we always used to hire a cottage in England for a couple of weeks, somewhere by the sea. Dad wasn't really that keen on going abroad. It was only when Mum got in touch with my grandparents, when I was about eight, that we went to visit them in Arizona.'

'Arizona?'

She blew out a breath. 'Um, that's the other reason Dad's a bit overprotective of me. Mum's not actually my birth mother—she met him when I was three and I was in her class at nursery school.'

'So your dad was a single parent?' he asked.

'My birth mother didn't abandon me, if that's what you're thinking. Not from choice, anyway.'

She bit her lip. 'Ajei died from complications the day after I was born.'

'Ah-heh?' The name wasn't familiar to him at all.

'Ajei. My birth mother.' She swallowed hard. 'She had a pulmonary embolism. There was nothing they could do.'

He realised that their fingers were still linked—how had that happened?—and he squeezed her hand. 'Sorry. That's tough on you, and I'm being intrusive.'

'No, it's fine. I'm OK talking about it. Obviously I never knew Ajei, but I've seen pictures of her, and in every single one she's smiling and looking happy. She's the one who named me Nizhoni.'

'I'd never even heard the name before I met you,' he said.

'You probably wouldn't, outside a certain area of America,' she said. 'It's Navajo—my mum's family's language. It means "beautiful". It's the first thing she said when she saw me, and she wanted it to be my name.'

'That's lovely.' He squeezed her hand again. 'So your mother was a Navajo?'

'The tribe's actually known as Diné, meaning "the people",' she said. 'But yes. She was an art student, training to be a silversmith. The jewellery she made was just gorgeous, all turquoise and silver. Dad was studying for a year in America after graduating from art school over here, and he met my mum at art college in LA. They fell in love, and then I came along.' She blew out a breath. 'I wasn't planned, and my grandparents weren't too pleased. But Ajei was their only child and they wanted her to be happy.'

Her fingers tightened round his. 'When she died, there was a huge row between my grandparents and my dad. Dad blamed them for encouraging my mum to have a home birth because they might've saved her in hospital; and my grandparents blamed him for getting my mum pregnant in the first place. They were all grieving, all angry about their loss, and they just couldn't see each other's point of view.'

'It must've been hard for all of them,' Aaron said.

'It was. Dad decided he'd had enough of the fighting and walked out—he left America and brought me straight home to England. And, until Mum persuaded him to try building a few bridges, he had no contact with my grandparents at all after he walked out.'

'Your mum sounds like a very special person. Both of your mothers, that is,' he said.

'They are. Ajei—her name means "my heart", and it's the first thing my grandmother said when she held her baby for the very first time—was special. Dad said there was something about her that always made him feel as if the sun had just risen. And Marianna's brilliant. She's always treated me as her daughter—she's never made me feel like the unwanted stepkid, not even when she had the boys,' Joni said.

'That's why Josie Stone's death hit you so hard,' he said. 'Because she was the stepchild, like you.'

She sighed. 'Yes. The sad thing is, I think Mrs Stone wanted to love Josie like her own—the way Mum loves me and I love her—but being a teenage girl is hard at the best of times. I guess it was easier for Josie to push her away.' She paused. 'And, with Ruby blaming herself for

Josie getting the plague—that must've hit a sore spot for you, too.'

It had. And he didn't want to talk about it. 'You were telling me about your grandparents,' he said, hoping to distract her further. 'So how did your mum get them talking to your dad again?'

'She convinced Dad that I really needed to know where I came from, and that my grandparents needed to know me. They'd already lost their only child and it wasn't fair to keep their only grandchild from them, too. I guess he felt a bit guilty, because he agreed. So she tracked them down from the last address he had for them, managed to find someone on the Internet who could get in touch with them, and sent them a picture of me. They asked if I could come to meet them—if all of us would come to Arizona. Dad was worried that they'd end up fighting again, but in the end they apologised to each other and made it up.' He could hear the smile in her voice. 'So I spend a couple of weeks in Arizona every year to catch up with my other family. *Shimá sání* has the Internet now, so we can Skype once a week and send emails, too.'

'Shimma what?' he asked.

'Shih-mah tsah-nih,' Joni said slowly. 'Basically that means my maternal grandmother.'

'In Navajo?' he guessed. 'You actually speak Navajo?'

'Only a little bit. I probably couldn't translate a whole conversation between English and Navajo, but I know the important stuff. My family's names, "I love you", that sort of thing.' She paused. 'Actually, one of my great-great-uncles was a Navajo code talker in the Second World War.'

'What's a code talker?' he asked.

'They were the people who encoded messages. They created a code that was never broken by the enemy. And they were really fast—it took them about twenty seconds to encode, transmit and decode a three-line message in English, whereas the code machines of the time would take about thirty minutes to do the same thing,' she said, sounding immensely proud.

He was stunned. 'That's amazing to have something like that in your family.'

'The Diné are amazing,' she said. 'And I'm really proud of my family.'

'I would be, too, in your shoes.' He paused. 'And your heritage explains your incredible hair.'

'You actually like my hair?'

'Yes. Why do you sound so surprised?'

'Bccause...' She sighed. 'It's complicated. And I owe you an apology.'

'For what?' He was mystified.

'About that night. The salsa club. I'm a bit ashamed about it because I, um, kind of used you.'

He really wasn't following. 'Used me? How?'

'To block out my wedding day.'

CHAPTER SEVEN

'YOU CAME HOME with me the night you got *married*?' Aaron began to think that he was in some kind of parallel universe. No way would someone like Joni Parker get married, dump her new husband and go off with a complete stranger that very evening. She just wouldn't.

Then again, she *had* told him that she was celebrating something, when he'd asked why she was drinking champagne...

He shook his head to clear it. 'No. That's just not the sort of thing you'd do. And I can't see you jilting someone at the altar, either.'

'I didn't jilt him or get married. It was just the day,' she explained. 'The one when I was supposed to get married, except it didn't happen.'

'And you were trying to block it out?'

'Yes.'

He could hear in her voice that she was upset.

And if your colleague was upset, the kind thing to do would be to put your arms round her and give her a hug, wouldn't it? It didn't mean he was getting *involved*. He ignored the fact that when she'd been upset after Josie Stone's death on the ward, he hadn't hugged her then.

Besides, it was cold in the damp, dark tunnel, so pulling Joni onto his lap and wrapping his arms round her was also the sensible thing to do, he told himself. Sharing body heat. It had everything to do with being practical and nothing at all with emotions. Nothing at all. Nothing at all to do with the fact that her warmth and sweetness drew him to her, made him want things he'd never wanted before. And he really wasn't sure whether it scared or thrilled him most.

She leaned her head against his shoulder, and he automatically stroked her hair. Her gorgeous, silky hair. Hair that he could remember falling across his face as she'd straddled him…

Though it really wasn't a good idea to let himself remember that. Or the way she'd made him feel. Because he couldn't afford to let himself feel things. Hadn't he learned from Ned's death that getting close to someone just led to pain and loneliness? 'For what it's worth, I think he was an idiot for dumping you,' he said.

She gave a mirthless laugh. 'He didn't dump me. I was the one who broke it off.'

He winced. 'Sorry. I didn't meant to put my foot in it.'

'But you assumed that I was the dumpee.'

'Joni, I know I've worked with you for less than a month, but I've seen the way you are with people. You're not the sort who'd trample over someone's feelings or be selfish,' he said. 'That's why I assumed that you were the one who got hurt.'

'Thank you for the vote of confidence,' she said dryly.

He knew he shouldn't ask. Especially as he had no intention of sharing his own situation. But it was as if his mouth wasn't in step with the programme. 'What happened?'

'He was offered a job. It meant moving to the other end of the country, so I wouldn't get to see much of my family.'

'And you might've had to change specialty,'

Aaron said, 'if the local hospital didn't have a tropical medicine department.'

'The firm he worked for had branches all over the country. I asked if he could negotiate, find out if he could do the same job in a branch within London instead of at the other end of the country,' Joni said. 'I wouldn't have minded a longer commute here every day.'

As long as she'd still been near her family, he guessed. 'And they couldn't do it?'

'He said not, though I wonder now if he ever even asked. According to Marty, it was his dream job. If I'd said that I didn't want to leave London—I didn't want to leave my family, my friends and my job—then he would've accused me of putting my family before him.'

'But he was asking you to put him before your family and your career. To put his needs before yours.'

'Yes. And I didn't think marriage was supposed to be like that. I thought it was supposed to be about compromise, about working together and finding something that works for both of you. Being a team,' she said. 'But Marty didn't like compromise. He liked things his way. And I was pretty spineless. I normally just went along with what he wanted. It seemed a bit—well—pointless and petty to make a fuss about all the little things.'

'What about the big things?' he asked softly.

'I agreed to go,' she said, and he noticed that she hadn't answered his question. 'I agreed to leave London and everyone here.'

He waited, knowing there was more and sure that she would fill the silence.

'And then,' she continued softly, 'he said that I should cut my hair. That it would look more professional and give me a better chance of getting a good job.'

'Apart from the fact you already have a good job, how on earth would cutting your hair make you look more professional?' Aaron asked, not understanding. 'Anyway, you always wear it back for work.'

'I think,' she said, 'it was just another hoop he wanted me to jump through. And I realised I didn't want to do that, only for him to want me to change something else. I wanted...' She sighed. 'It's going to sound wet, and I don't mean to complain. But I always manage to pick the wrong guy. I do my best to make it work, but eventually I realise that I'm the one making all the compromises and all the effort and he's really not that bothered. And I'm just not prepared to do that any more.'

'That sounds entirely reasonable,' Aaron said. And it was yet another reminder that he was wrong for her. She needed someone who could do the emotional stuff. Not him. 'I can't believe your ex actually expected you to cut your hair just because he wanted you to do it. It's your hair, and it's up to you how you wear it.'

'Exactly. I know it sounds petty, but there had been so many other little things. I guess that one was the last straw. It made me think about what I wanted from life—and I didn't want the life I saw opening up in front of me. I didn't want to marry Marty and get more and more miserable. So I called off the wedding.'

'That takes a lot of courage,' Aaron said. 'Once everything's set in motion and everyone's expecting the big day to happen, it's really hard to say that you've made a mistake and you've changed your mind. It's easier to go along with it and do what everyone expects you to do.'

'I almost did,' she said. 'We'd booked the church and the reception venue, ordered the flowers and the cars, chosen the food. We'd paid all the deposits.'

'Sometimes,' he said, 'there are more important things to think about than money. Sometimes it's more important to do the right thing.'

'That's what all my family and friends said, when I called it off. That I was doing the right thing,' Joni said. 'Marty didn't get along with Bailey, either, so I only ever got to see her for lunch in the hospital cafeteria towards the end. And even then I'd tell him I had lunch with friends and not be specific about who, to avoid a row. He didn't want her to be my bridesmaid— he wanted his sister to be my only bridesmaid.'

'Your ex sounds like a total control freak,' Aaron said.

'He wasn't, at first. He was a sweetheart when I met him. But then he changed, little by little.'

Little things leading to bigger things. 'Maybe

he got confident enough to stop hiding who he really was,' Aaron suggested.

'That's what Bailey said.'

'Wise,' he said. He'd only exchanged a couple of words with Joni's best friend at the salsa club, but the more he heard about her the more he liked her.

'It was Bailey's idea to go to the salsa club to celebrate my lucky escape. She said we could either stay at home and eat our body weight in junk food and ice cream and then feel gross the next morning—and it would seriously mess up my blood sugar, so she didn't recommend it— or we could go and dance ourselves happy.' Joni laughed. 'She's a sports medicine specialist, so she's a great believer in endorphins. According to her, exercise makes *everything* better.'

He couldn't help smiling. 'She has a point. When I've had a tough shift, going for a run always makes me feel better.'

'I wasn't actually looking to start something with someone that night,' Joni said. 'But I'd had a glass of champagne, and because of my diabetes I don't drink very often, so the bubbles went to my head. I guess it makes me a bit of a cheap date.'

Aaron laughed. 'There's absolutely nothing cheap about you, Joni Parker. I wasn't looking to start something with anyone, either. You and me…it just happened.'

'And we've agreed it was a one-off,' she said quickly.

'Absolutely.' So why did that make him feel disappointed? He should've felt relieved. Happy, even. His head really wasn't in the right place for a relationship. And sitting here with her on his lap and his arms wrapped round her was a really bad idea. Except he couldn't think of a way to back off without hurting her—and he didn't want to do that. Plus, if he was honest with himself, he *liked* sitting here with his arms wrapped round her. He liked holding her close.

'I'm not good at relationships,' he said. 'I don't do emotional stuff. So it never lasts beyond a few dates.'

'Maybe,' she said, 'you just haven't yet found the right person for you.'

'Do you actually believe that? That there's a Mr or Miss Right for everyone?' he asked.

'A soul mate, you mean?'

'Yes.'

She was silent for a while, obviously thinking about it. 'Yes. Though it isn't necessarily the person you think it's going to be, and it isn't necessarily just one person for the whole of your life. I mean, look at my dad—he was so young when my mum died. I don't think Ajei would've wanted him to be alone for the rest of his life, mourning her for the next fifty years or more. I think she would've wanted him to find someone who'd make him happy and who'd love me as her own. Which he did, when he met Marianna, and I'm really glad.'

'And that's what you're looking for?' he asked. 'Mr Right?'

'Right now,' she said, 'I'm not looking for anyone at all. And I'm sorry I used you to block out my wedding day.'

'Don't apologise.' He kept his arms round her. 'I think what happened was down to both of us.'

'It wasn't meant to happen. I planned just to

have a glass or two of champagne and dance myself silly.'

But then he'd asked her to dance. And the moment of attraction across a crowded floor had suddenly got a whole lot more complex.

Just as right now had suddenly got a whole lot more complex. She was in his arms, sitting on his lap, and her face was only centimetres away from his. All he had to do was turn very slightly, dip his head very slightly, and his mouth would connect with hers.

He knew it would be the wrong thing to do. Joni wanted someone who'd make her happy— and he was rubbish at emotional stuff. He'd end up hurting her just as much as her ex had.

But, even as the thought bloomed in his head, he found himself moving closer. Touching his mouth to hers, brushing so lightly across it that his skin tingled.

Once wasn't enough.

He did it again, and his mouth tingled some more.

'Aaron,' she said, her voice sweet and soft and inviting.

The next thing he knew, her hands were in his hair, his arms were wrapped tightly round her, and she was kissing him back. Hot, urgent, desperate.

Hell. This had to stop.

He broke the kiss. 'Joni,' he said hoarsely, 'I'm sorry. I shouldn't have done that.'

'Uh-huh.' Her voice went all cool, and she wriggled on his lap, clearly trying to put some space between them.

'I didn't...' Oh, hell. 'I've never been inarticulate in my life,' he said, 'but I am with you, and I'm making a total mess of this.'

She stopped wriggling. 'So what are you saying, Aaron?'

'I'm saying I wish I was different,' he said. 'There's a big part of me that wants to ask you to see where this thing between us goes. But that wouldn't be fair to you. As I said, I'm not good at emotional stuff. And I don't want to hurt you, Joni. Just as I'm betting that you've already been hurt enough and you don't want to risk it, either.'

'Hey. I've picked myself up and dusted myself down,' she said. 'I'm not letting what happened with Marty affect the rest of my life. Well, I'm trying not to,' she said. 'And when I meet the right person, I'll learn to trust again.'

'Good.' And how sad was it that part of him really wished he could be that right person?

'You know, *shimá sání* always told me that I could be whoever I wanted to be,' she said.

Where was she going with this?

'You just said, you wished you were different. Which means you want to be.' She paused. 'Which means you *could* be.'

Was she suggesting that they could see where this thing between them was going? That they could take the risk—together?

The tightness across Aaron's shoulders eased a little. And, even though they were sitting in the pitch dark, weirdly everything seemed a tiny bit brighter.

'I like you, Aaron,' she said.

He liked her, too, but he wouldn't say it. Because how could he ask her to take a huge emotional risk on someone who was such a mess inside?

'You're a good doctor,' she continued. 'From

what I've seen you're kind to the patients, you're easy to work with, and you're good at teaching the junior staff and giving them confidence in their abilities.'

'Thank you. So are you,' he said, meaning it.

'Thank you.' She paused. 'And you're hot.'

He didn't quite believe she'd said that. 'I'm what?'

'You heard. I'm not repeating it.'

'Are you propositioning me, Joni Parker?'

'That's your flaw, Mr Hughes,' she said. 'You're just a tiny bit slow on the uptake.' But there was laughter in her voice. She was teasing him, not criticising or condemning.

'So you *are* propositioning me.'

'Right now, I'm sitting on your lap and your arms are wrapped around me,' she pointed out.

'Because we're in a damp, cold place and this is the most efficient way for us both to keep warm.'

She'd obviously worked out that it was all an excuse—little more than bravado—because she asked, 'So you'd be sitting here exactly like this if you were stuck here with another colleague from the department?'

'Sure,' he lied.

'Even if it was Mikey or Mr Flinders?'

He pressed his cheek against hers. 'OK. Maybe not if it was Mikey or Mr Flinders.'

She laughed. 'Well, then. I'm just saying, you could be that different person.' She paused. 'If you wanted to.'

Could he?

The temptation was so strong.

'So you'd take a risk on me if I asked you out? Even though I don't have a good track record with relationships?'

She kissed the very corner of his mouth. 'There's only one way to find out, isn't there?'

CHAPTER EIGHT

JONI KNEW SHE was taking a huge risk and this could all blow up in her face. If she'd got this wrong…well, it would be awkward and embarrassing at work for a couple of weeks, but eventually they'd move past it, she told herself. And if she'd got it right…

Oh, please let her have got this right.

'Be the person I want to be,' Aaron said, as if mulling it over. 'Joni, I need to be fair with you. I'm not good at relationships, apart from professional ones with my patients and colleagues. I'm not even that good at having friends. I never have been. I get on fine with people and I fit in OK, but I don't know how to be close to people. And I'm a total disaster area when it comes to emotional stuff.' He blew out a breath. 'But, despite all that, would you consider having dinner with me some time?'

'Just to be clear—you're asking me out on a date?' she asked.

'Yes. I'm asking you out on a date,' he said softly.

'We've both been hurt in the past, made mistakes,' she said, equally softly. 'I'm probably just as much a disaster area as you when it comes to relationships. But, yes, I'd like to go on a proper date with you. I'd love to have dinner with you.'

'Good.' He kissed the corner of her mouth, and it made her feel hot all over. All she could concentrate on was the warmth of his arms around her and the softness of his lips. A couple of minutes ago, they'd been kissing each other desperately, everything happening at a rate of knots. Now the pace had shifted to slow and unbearably sweet. And the possibility of how good it could be between them left her breathless.

'So we'll take it slowly,' she said.

She could feel him smiling against her mouth. 'I guess we started with things rather the wrong way round.'

Joni was really glad that they were in complete darkness, otherwise she knew her face would be beetroot red to betray her shame. 'Just so you know, I don't normally get drunk and go off with complete strangers I've only just met on the dance floor.'

'I know I'm a little slow on the uptake,' he said, 'but I'd already worked that one out for myself. And, just so *you* know, I don't normally go dancing and take complete strangers home with me, either.'

'I'm glad to hear it.'

'Though,' he said, his voice deepening, 'I don't regret taking you home with me at all. Except for one thing.'

Joni went very still, thinking of the way Marty had started to change once they'd begun dating. All her doubts came rushing back. Was she just about to make the same stupid mistake all over again and start a relationship with someone who wouldn't put as much effort in as she did? He'd practically warned her off. She'd been an idiot, refusing to listen. Would she never learn? 'What's that?' she asked carefully.

'That I sleep like the dead—otherwise I would've heard you get up in the morning. I would've made you a coffee before you left, and hopefully persuaded you to stay for breakfast.'

She relaxed again. 'Oh.'

'And,' he said, 'about that dinner date…I think I'd like a breakfast date some time, too.'

'Breakfast,' she said, 'isn't exactly taking things slowly.'

'It is if we don't spend the night together first—say if we meet somewhere for breakfast,' he pointed out. 'And I'd like that. To spend a whole day with you, getting to know you better. Finding out what makes you tick.'

In answer, she kissed him.

By the time she broke the kiss, they were both shaking.

'And this is just between you and me, right?' she asked. 'As far as work's concerned, we're just colleagues—not because I'm ashamed of dating you or anything like that, but because it stops things getting complicated.'

'Agreed,' he said. 'Though I reserve the right to sneak a kiss in the corridor when nobody's looking.'

She laughed. 'Aaron, you make me feel like a teenager again. And I'm thirty years old.'

'Snap. On the teenager bit,' he said. 'Though you have a few years on me. I'm thirty-three.'

'That's quite young, for a consultant.' She stroked his face. 'Which means you're clever. Geeky, even.' She stole another kiss. 'And that T-shirt you were wearing when we went rock-climbing on the departmental night out gives you extra points. I like your sense of humour.'

'Good.' He paused. 'Speaking of the departmental night out…I hope you realise I had a bad time that evening. All because of your jeans.'

'Because of my jeans?' She didn't understand. 'Why?'

'Because I wanted to be on my own with you in a very private place so I could peel them off you. Very, very slowly,' he said. 'So if I was a bit offish with anyone that evening, now you know why. I was trying to keep my imagination and my libido under control.'

'Uh-huh.' And now he'd put ideas into her imagination. Ideas that were rapidly spiralling out of control. So much for taking this slowly.

Aaron Hughes made her temperature and her pulse spike.

He kissed her again. 'So. You and me. For now, until we know where it's going, it's just between us. And I think we need to change the subject and talk about something really serious and work-related, because otherwise it could be really embarrassing when they dig us out of here and we look as if we've been kissing each other stupid.'

He was right. She knew that. It would be sensible to put some distance between them. Even though she didn't want to move because she liked being in his arms. 'I guess I'd better, um, move.'

His arms stayed wrapped right round her. 'I didn't quite mean that. Besides, this is efficient sharing of body heat.'

Oh. So he didn't want her to move, either. 'Uh-huh,' she said.

'Talk to me about work. You know why I went into tropical medicine. What about you?'

'Because that way I get to hear about all the exciting places where my patients have visited,' she said, laughing. 'Which is horribly shallow of me. But I also like the research side, and I really love the idea of helping to eradicate a disease or find a vaccine to help prevent it in the first place.' She paused. 'Funnily enough, *shimá sání* is a bit—well, fey, I guess you'd say. She said when my mum was pregnant with me, she knew I'd be a healer.'

'You mean, like a shaman?' he asked.

'Maybe, if I'd grown up on the reservation in Arizona. Though in my mum's language it's not shaman, it's *hataŧii*.'

'Ha'atathli,' he said, trying to copy her pronunciation. 'Could you still be one now?'

'No,' she said. 'You need to be apprenticed at a really young age because there's so much to learn and it's not written down—everything's passed down orally from one generation to the next, and it's obviously all in Navajo and I don't speak enough of it. Though I would've had someone to be apprenticed to. *Shi cheii*— my grandfather—is a *hataŧii*,' she said.

'Your grandfather's a healer? So what happened to your mum…' He blew out a breath.

'That must've made things even harder for your family to handle.'

'Yes. That's why the row was so bad,' she said. 'Dad and *shi cheii* both felt guilty that their way had failed, and it made them really lash out at each other.'

'So, as a qualified doctor, you're caught in the middle between them?'

'Actually, no,' she said. '*Shi cheii* is really proud that I've followed in his footsteps—only obviously in my father's culture rather than my mother's. And I have great discussions with him about medicine and how he'd treat someone compared with the way I would. I think we've learned a lot from each other. In Diné culture, it's very much holistic medicine—it's about restoring *hózhǫ* to the patient.'

'What's ho-joh?' Aaron asked.

'*Hózhǫ* means harmony—I guess you could call it order, because it's about putting everything in balance, not just curing the symptoms. Holistic medicine, really. So the *hataɫii* will spend time talking to the patient, finding out everything that's wrong and that's worrying them.'

'And if a patient talks, and feels they're being listened to, that's a good thing,' Aaron said. 'It reduces a lot of the worry and stress.'

'Exactly. And think how many illnesses have stress as their root cause,' Joni continued. 'Teaching people to restore the balance in their life can help with that, too.'

'So it's all psychological?'

'No, there's some herbal medicine, too. Apprentices start by making up medicine bundles, mainly herbs. Some are made into tinctures, some are burned.'

'And I'm guessing that if you broke them down into their chemical composition, there would be similarities with Western medicines?' Aaron asked.

'Yes. Actually, I've got a research proposal with Mr Flinders at the moment, looking into alternatives to antibiotics that might exist in Native American medicine.'

'That sounds really interesting,' Aaron said. 'With more bacteria becoming resistant to the antibiotics we have now, we really need to look at alternatives because we only have a few more years left while they'll still work, and then we'll be right back to where we started in the years before penicillin was discovered, where people can die from scratching themselves on a thorn. Tell me more.'

Joni found herself telling him all about her pet project.

'For what it's worth, you've got my backing,' he said when she'd finished. 'And if I can do anything to help, I'd love to be involved. It sounds fascinating.'

'Thank you. I might well take you up on that,' Joni said.

Right then, Aaron's stomach growled. 'Sorry. It feels like a long time since we had that tea and biscuits,' he said.

'What's the time?'

'I'll check my phone.' Light glowed in the tunnel, giving Aaron's face a ghostly air as he checked the time on his phone. 'It's nearly lunchtime.'

'Because of the diabetes, I always carry snacks with me,' she said. 'I have a couple of cereal bars and a bag of jelly babies in my pocket. We can share them.'

'No, you need to eat them,' he said. 'Don't worry about me. I can live with being a bit hungry, but I don't want your blood sugar crashing. Do you need to check your blood glucose? I can put the torch on for a bit, so you can see what you're doing.'

'Thanks. I have to admit, I'm starting to feel as if my blood sugar's getting a bit low.' She tested herself while he held the torch steady. 'Yes, it's dropping a bit. I could do with some carbs.' She fished the jelly babies out of her pocket and offered the bag to him.

'Thanks, but, honestly, I'm fine,' he said, and stroked her face. 'You need them more than I do. Although the rest of the group must have worked out that we're missing by now, they still have to find us and we don't know how long we're going to be stuck in here.'

'I'm on insulin twice a day,' she said, 'but I don't need to take any until this evening. These and the cereal bar will keep me going for a few more hours. Though I still feel bad about eating and you not having anything.'

He kissed her lightly. 'There's a medical reason for it, so don't feel bad. Put it this way, I'd feel an awful lot worse if I ate your food and you had a hypo while we're trapped in a tunnel and I couldn't do anything to help you. So will you please stop stressing and just eat?'

'Point taken,' she said, and ate a handful of the jelly babies and one of the cereal bars. Though she was relieved that Aaron did at least accept a couple of mouthfuls from the bottle of water she also carried with her.

'Did you hear that?' Aaron asked a while later. 'Someone's shouting outside.'

'You think they've worked out where we are?' Joni asked.

'I hope so. After three, if we both yell "hello" as loud as we can, they've got more chance of hearing us. And they'll know it's a voice making the noise rather than just a stone falling or something.'

'Agreed,' Joni said.

He counted them in, and they both yelled, 'Hello!'

There was a yell back from outside.

'We're in here,' Aaron called. 'The roof fell in.'

The words from outside were muffled, but he could just about work them out: 'We're making it safe and digging you out.'

'We need to move back a bit further,' he said to Joni, 'in case their digging triggers another roof fall.'

'Do we get some light, this time?' she asked.

'Good idea,' he said.

It took their rescuers another hour to build a stable tunnel to get them out, and just as Aaron had feared there were a couple more roof falls in the meantime, but finally they could see daylight coming in from the outside.

'Come out one at a time, and try not to dislodge anything on your way out,' a voice Aaron recognised as that of the team leader called.

'You first,' he told Joni. 'And don't argue.'

Waiting in the tunnel, knowing that the entrance could easily fall in again and trap him alone in the dark—just as he'd been all those years ago when the house had been bombed—stretched his nerves to the limit. But at last Joni was through, and it was his turn to crawl through the makeshift tunnel.

'We were so worried when you didn't get back,' Nancy said. 'We tried ringing your mobile, Joni, but it kept saying you were unavailable. We thought one or both of you might have fallen and been hurt.'

'Just a roof fall blocking our way out. We're fine,' Aaron said lightly. 'No injuries of any description, and Joni had some carbs on her so her blood sugar's OK, too.'

'We couldn't call anyone from the tunnel because we didn't have a signal on our phones,' Joni said. 'We just hoped you'd realise something was wrong when we didn't come back and would come and find us.'

'We searched for you for an hour before we found you,' the team leader said. Joni produced the small box from her pocket. 'We did get the final clue, by the way. We just couldn't call it in because of the signal problem.'

'I think you can be forgiven,' the team leader

said. 'Come on, let's get you back to base and get you warmed up. It must have been freezing in there.'

'Just a tad,' Joni said with a smile.

And was it his imagination, Aaron wondered, or was she blushing ever so slightly? Because there had been quite a few moments when neither of them had been aware of the temperature...

Back at base, they had hot drinks and a cooked meal, and then there was a final set of team-building exercises.

'I think,' Mikey said when they were on the way back to the hospital at the end of the day, 'we can definitely say we all bonded today. We were that worried about you two.'

'We were just lucky that the tunnel entrance collapsed when we were nowhere near it,' Joni said.

'All the same, we'll be raising a glass to you both at the next departmental night out,' Nancy said. 'Actually, that reminds me, Aaron—the next one's already organised, but can I put you down to organise the one after that?'

'Sure,' he said with a smile.

Maybe here in London it would be different.

And he could be different, too. Learn to do emotional stuff.

CHAPTER NINE

LATER THAT EVENING, Aaron called Joni. 'Hi.'

'Hi.'

Help. What did he say now? His social skills seemed to have completely deserted him. Which was utterly ridiculous. 'I, um, was just wondering how you were.'

'I'm fine,' she said. 'All the lights in my flat are on and I've checked everywhere for spiders.'

'That's good.' He paused. Oh, for pity's sake. This was worse than being a teenager again, asking out the girl you didn't think you had a chance with. Though he'd already done that bit, hadn't he? In principle. And this call was meant to be about specifics. He pulled himself together and made an effort. 'You know we talked about having dinner—I was wondering when you might be free.'

'How about Friday?' she suggested.

'That works for me, too. OK. I'll book something.' And now he was back in his comfort zone. 'Is there any food you really hate, or do you have any allergies?'

'No allergies, and I like just about everything except offal and chocolate,' she said. 'I really don't mind where we go, as long as I know the dress code.'

'Sure. I'll find something and text you later, OK?'

'OK. And, Aaron?'

'Yes,' he said warily.

'I'm really glad you called.'

Funny how that made him feel all warm inside. He wasn't used to feeling like this, and it scared him as much as it made him feel good. 'Yeah. See you tomorrow,' he mumbled, and ended the call.

He spent a while browsing the Internet, trying to find a restaurant he thought Joni would enjoy. Nothing too casual, because he wanted to her feel that he'd thought about it and was trying to make the evening special for her; but nothing too fussy where they wouldn't get a chance to talk.

In the end, he chanced upon something a little bit different.

It would be a risk. Especially for an official first date.

He rang to see if there were any spaces left. They were full, but they'd just had a cancellation so two places had become free. This was fate, he told himself, and booked it.

Then he texted Joni.

Booked for Friday. Meet at the tube station near your flat, six p.m. Dressy, but wear shoes you can walk in.

She texted back within moments.

OK. Where are we going?

Surprise, he texted back. She didn't need to know that it was going to be a surprise for him, too—did she?

Dressy, but wear shoes you can walk in. Which told her absolutely nothing, other than that they were going to have to walk from the tube station to the restaurant. But shoes she could walk in just didn't go with her dress. So did she wear flats until they got to the restaurant, and change her shoes then? Or…

She texted Aaron.

I could book us a taxi, if you like.

And then he'd have to tell her where they were going instead of keeping it as a 'surprise', right?

No. We have to take the tube, he replied.

What? Why? She had absolutely no idea, and if she texted him she knew he wouldn't give her a proper answer, so she gave up and rang him. 'Why do we have to take the tube?'

'I'll explain on Friday.'

She sighed. 'You like playing the Man of Mystery, don't you?'

'Maybe.'

'Arrgh,' she said in frustration, and he laughed.

'By the way—do you prefer red or white wine?' he asked.

'Either. Why?'

'More Man of Mystery stuff,' he said, and she groaned again.

Aaron refused to be drawn about what was really happening on Friday night when she asked him at work, too, so Joni was none the wiser by the time Friday evening arrived.

Dressy.

So that would be her little black dress—demure, knee-length and very plain. Flats to walk in, the red high heels she'd worn at the salsa club to change into when they got there—wherever 'there' was—and her mother's turquoise choker, she decided. Hair most definitely down, and her usual bare minimum of make-up teamed with a spritz of her favourite perfume; and she was at the tube station near to her flat at exactly six o'clock.

Aaron was waiting outside, leaning against the wall, and he was attracting second glances from just about every woman who passed. Which was hardly surprising, she thought; in a dark suit, white shirt and a plain deep red silk tie, he looked stunning.

And he was all hers.

It made her feel like a teenage girl on her first date with the coolest boy in school. Except she and Aaron had already gone way beyond the first date. Before they'd even been dating.

And now they'd agreed to take it slowly. Get to know each other better outside work. Tonight was their first date. Just the thought of it made her tingle all over with anticipation and excitement. Yet, at the same time, it scared her witless. Given the mess her last relationship had become, and the fact that Aaron had been very frank with her about being hopeless with emotional stuff, was she doing the right thing? Was she setting herself up for yet another fall?

To cover her doubts, she walked over to him and gave him her brightest smile. 'Hi,' she said, and kissed him on the cheek. And then she grimaced. 'Sorry. I've just covered you in lipstick.' She grabbed a tissue from her handbag and dabbed the lipstick off his skin.

He just smiled. 'You look gorgeous. And I'm glad you wore your hair down.'

'Thank you.' She felt the colour seeping into her face. To cover her embarrassment, she asked,

'So now I'm here, where are we actually going, oh Man of Mystery?'

'Right at this moment,' he said, 'I don't actually know.'

She blinked, surprised. 'But you said you'd booked somewhere.'

'I have.'

She still didn't understand. 'So why don't you know where we're going?'

'Because it's a surprise supper club,' he explained. 'The venue changes every week—we've booked for tonight and I should get a text any minute now to tell us where to go.'

Now she understood why he'd asked her to wear shoes she could walk in. 'So it's like a pop-up restaurant crossed with a magical mystery tour?' She smiled. 'What a fabulous idea.'

He looked visibly relieved. 'It's a bit of a risk—especially for a first date—because I have absolutely no clue what the venue's going to be like. But apparently the food's fantastic. The only thing is, there's a set menu so you don't get a choice, and you have to bring your own wine because they don't have a licence to sell alcohol.'

'Which is why you asked me if I preferred red or white wine.'

He gestured to the carrier bag he was holding. 'I played it safe. I hope you like Sauvignon Blanc.'

'I do.' She smiled. 'This is so exciting. I've always wanted to go to a pop-up restaurant.'

'We were really lucky. Someone had cancelled just before I called, so we managed to get the last two places.'

'Obviously it was meant to be,' she said.

His phone beeped, and he read the text. 'We get off the train three stops from here, and then we'll get more directions.'

'And at least this treasure hunt isn't going to end in a tunnel that collapses on us,' she said, laughing.

He frowned. 'Actually, for all I know we *might* end up in a tunnel. Would that be a problem?'

'No, because it wouldn't be like the one on the team-building day.'

The guarded look left his face. 'Let's go, then.'

They took the train as directed, and then followed the directions in a series of texts. The last one sent them down a flight of narrow stairs to a basement room, where a waiter in a burgundy bow tie and black tailcoat handed them a glass of something sparkling and directed them through to the next room.

'It's a wine cellar,' she said as they passed rack upon rack of dusty bottles. She took a sip from her glass. 'Elderflower cordial. That's lovely— really summery.'

The next room took her breath away; there were tiny bistro tables laid out in the wine cellar, with white damask tablecloths, sparkling silverware and fresh flowers. The whole place was lit by candlelight alone.

'This so romantic,' she said softly. 'Thank you for booking this, Aaron. I've never been anywhere so lovely.'

Joni didn't think it could get better than that but, just after the waitress had seated them and uncorked their wine, a group of four musicians—all in tailcoats and white bow ties and carrying a cello, a violin or a viola—came in and sat down in the corner. As soon as they started playing, she recognised the melody.

'Oh, I love this—Pachelbel's *Canon*,' she said. 'So we get great live music as well as great food? Aaron, this is utterly perfect.'

'I'm glad you like it.'

He still seemed a little tense, so she lifted her wineglass. 'To us,' she said, 'and seeing where this takes us—whether it ends up being a good friendship or something more.'

For a moment, she didn't think he was going to respond. And then he smiled—a smile that actually reached his eyes. Clearly he was as nervous about this whole thing as she was. 'To us,' he echoed.

'Given that you're a coffee geek, would I be right in thinking you're a foodie, too?' she asked.

'A bit,' he admitted. 'I know my way round a kitchen, and I'm comfortable experimenting. You?'

'The same—though I'm very boring on Monday nights. Bailey and I always go out for dinner to the same restaurant after our yoga class— and, although we've worked our way through the entire menu over the last year or so, we're a bit, um, predictable with our order nowadays,' she confessed.

He smiled. 'There's nothing wrong with having favourites.'

The food turned out to be as fabulous as Aaron had hoped—beetroot risotto, followed by salmon served on a bed of puy lentils with finely shredded Savoy cabbage.

'Definitely cooked in butter, lemon and chilli,' Joni said after she'd tasted the greens. 'What a fabulous mixture.'

'I agree,' Aaron said.

The Eton mess with raspberries served with the thinnest, lightest shortbread rounds were perfect, and then finally coffee—which lived up to Aaron's standards—and petits fours, including the thinnest slice of orange Joni had ever seen. 'That must have been cut with a mandolin,' she said.

Aaron took a bite of his. 'And it's been caramelised.'

'Without changing the colour? That's amazing,' she said, and tried hers. 'That's seriously impressive. Thank you, Aaron,' she said. 'This is the nicest meal I've had in a very long time.' She looked thoughtful. 'Do you think the organisers would do a one-off pop-up for a group?'

'They might do. Are you thinking I could book them for the departmental night out Nancy wants me to organise?' he asked.

'I think the team would love it. And if the organisers can find somewhere really different, you might just beat my rainstorm as the most unusual night out ever.'

'That sounds like a challenge,' Aaron said.

She raised an eyebrow. 'It might be.'

'So, if I meet your challenge, what are the stakes?'

'We can start at a kiss,' she said.

'Start at a kiss—and finish where?'

Even the thought left her breathless. 'Um— Woman of Mystery stuff?' she suggested, and he laughed.

They chatted to the organiser after the event. 'We really enjoyed ourselves tonight,' Aaron said, 'and we were wondering if you would be able to organise an event for a team night out?'

'How many people?' the organiser asked.

Aaron looked at Joni.

'About fifteen,' Joni said.

'That's doable,' the organiser said. 'I'll need to check my diary so I can give you a date—is that OK?'

'That's great. We tend to organise it for the middle of the week so most of us can make it,' Joni explained, 'and usually we do something before we eat.'

'Or you could include the entertainment as part of the night,' the organiser suggested. 'One of my clients runs a circus school, so maybe we could serve the meal in a marquee and you and your colleagues could do a bit of tightrope walking and juggling beforehand. And my client could ask some of his troupe to do an act in between the main course and pudding.'

Aaron and Joni looked at each other.

'That,' Aaron said, 'would be absolutely perfect.'

When they'd finished making arrangements, Aaron called a taxi. Joni's flat was on the way to his, so he dropped her there first, asking the taxi driver to wait while he saw her safely inside.

'You're very welcome to come in for a cup of tea,' Joni said, 'but no way am I going to dare to offer you a coffee.'

He laughed. 'I'm not that picky.'

Her expression said that she begged to differ.

And he wasn't quite ready for the evening to end yet. 'A cup of tea would be lovely,' he said. 'I'll just pay the taxi driver.'

'I'll put the kettle on,' she said.

Joni's flat was pretty much what Aaron had expected. Like her, the decor was warm and vibrant. The kitchen was painted a bright sunshiny yellow, with maple cupboards and worktops; there was a shelf full of cookery books, and there were lots of photographs and postcards held to the fridge with magnets.

Clearly she'd seen his glance because she smiled. 'Knock yourself out.' She poured boiling water into the two mugs, then came back to talk him through the photographs. 'Bailey, you already know. That's Olly on stage with his band, Luke in Rome because he says the Pantheon roof is the most perfect piece of architectural engineering ever and he has to visit it at least once a year so he can drool over it, and Mum and Dad.'

He could see the resemblance between Joni and her father, and between her brothers.

'This is *shi cheii* and *shimá sání*—my grandparents.' Both were wearing jeans and checked shirts, which surprised him, and clearly it showed in his face because Joni gave him a sidelong look. 'American Indians don't wear traditional clothes all the time, you know.'

'No. Of course not. Sorry.'

'And this is *shimá*—my mother, Ajei.'

The photograph was of a young woman with long dark hair, sitting on a rock against a bright blue sky, clearly pregnant and looking absolutely radiant. The picture of happiness, Aaron thought. 'She's beautiful. She looks so much like you.'

Joni inclined her head in acknowledgement. 'Thank you. Though I'm ten years older now than she is in that picture.'

He could see the sadness in her eyes. Not knowing what else to do, he gave her a hug.

She leaned against him briefly. 'Thank you,' she said softly. 'Come and sit down.'

Her living room was also painted a sunshiny yellow. There was a burnt-orange sofa with deep red cushions; the rug in the middle of floor was the same deep red as the cushions, with geometric designs woven into it. Again she clearly saw where he was looking. 'That rug was woven by one of my cousins. I brought it back from Arizona a couple of years ago.'

'Your cousin's a very talented weaver,' he said.

Joni smiled. 'I'll tell her that, the next time I talk to her.'

There were lots of family photographs on the mantelpiece, Aaron noticed, including Joni's graduation and those of her brothers, and a photograph of her parents' wedding with Joni cuddled between them as the bridesmaid. There was so much love in her family and everyone seemed so close. How could he ever be enough for her?

He pushed the panic away. Later. Not now. 'I meant to say earlier, I really like your necklace.'

She looked pleased. 'My mother made it.'

'It's beautiful—like you, Nizhoni.'

She blushed. *'Ahéhee.'*

'I'm guessing that's Navajo,' he said, 'but what does it mean?'

'Thank you,' she said with a smile.

'You're welcome,' he said, smiling back. 'Do you have much of your mother's jewellery?'

'I have another necklace, two bracelets and a ring,' she said. 'I gave some of the pieces to *shimá sání*, because I thought she really ought to have some of her daughter's work.'

'That's kind,' he said.

'Not really.' She shrugged. 'She's my grand-mother and I love her.'

So easy. Aaron thought of his own grandpar-ents—remote, on both sides. He'd stayed with them sometimes during school holidays, and he'd felt as much of a nuisance to them as he'd been to his parents. What must it be like to have such an easy relationship—to be close despite the geographical distance? His own family might as well have been in another solar system. And he hated the idea that it could hurt her.

'What are you thinking?' she asked softly.

No way was he admitting to any of that. 'The tunnel. The best thing about that day was holding you. And there's the fact that I met your challenge, earlier—the stakes, I believe, were a kiss.' And even the idea of it melted his self-control. Almost. He just about managed to let himself pause. 'May I?'

She stroked his face. 'Aaron, you're so sweet. I like the fact that you ask, you don't just assume.'

Well, good. But he needed to kiss her. Right now. Before he imploded. He coughed. 'Was that a yes or a no?'

'A definite yes.'

'Good.' He set her mug of tea on the floor next to his, and scooped her onto his lap. Funny how holding her made him feel so much better.

'I really had a great time tonight,' she said. 'Thank you for organising it.'

'It was a bit of a risk,' he admitted. 'If the venue or food had been awful…'

'Actually, it wouldn't have mattered,' she said, 'because you put a lot of thought into it and tried to make it a special evening, and that's the important thing.'

'So you've forgiven me for all the Man of Mystery stuff?' he asked.

'Ask me nicely, and I'll tell you,' she said with a teasing smile.

'All right. Please will you forgive me for the Man of Mystery stuff?'

She laughed. 'That's not quite what I meant by "nicely".'

'So I'm being slow on the uptake again?'

She grinned. 'Just a tad. Think about the stakes I owe you.'

He kissed her, long and slow and tender. Dragging it out, just because he really liked kissing her. And even though his head was yelling a warning that he shouldn't let his guard down, shouldn't let himself get involved, he couldn't stop himself. The feel of her skin against his. The soft floral scent she wore. The sound of his blood thrumming through his veins. The way she tasted.

And how incredibly hot she looked when he broke the kiss—her eyes all huge, her lips reddened and parted, and her head tipped back slightly in offering. It made him want to do it all over again. And again. And take it further, until she was falling apart under the touch of his hands and his mouth.

He'd never felt this kind of temptation before. It scared the hell out of him; and yet at the same time he wanted more, too.

'Now, that's what I call a kiss,' she said, and laughed up at him.

God, she was gorgeous. And he wanted her more than he'd ever wanted anyone in his life. 'So am I forgiven?' Or did he get to kiss her some more, until hopefully she was in as stupid a state as he was?

'You're forgiven,' she said. 'Just.'

'*Ahéhee*,' he said, and she laughed and kissed him until he was dizzy.

'So do you like other music apart from classical?' she asked.

'I like a pretty wide range of music,' he said, 'except maybe boy-band stuff.'

She smiled. 'That's because you're not a teenage girl. My brother's band is playing on

Wednesday night. A few of us from the department are going, as well as my family and Bailey—so I was wondering, would you like to come?'

It wasn't a 'meet the family' thing, then—more like a mini departmental night out. OK. He could cope with that. 'I'd like that very much,' he said, then paused. 'Um, would this be an exception to my "I don't really like boy bands" stance?'

'Absolutely not,' she said. 'Olly's band is a cross between rock and blues. They do some cover versions, but he writes a lot of their own songs.'

'Rock and blues? Now, that,' he said, 'so happens to be my favourite kind of music.' He named a few of the bands he liked.

'Olly loves them. Have you seen any of them live?'

'Manchester has a good music scene,' he said. 'So, yes—several times.'

'Then I think you and Olly are going to get on really, really well,' she said with a smile.

Although she didn't spell it out, he knew from what she'd said before that Marty hadn't got on that well with her family. Family wasn't every-thing—though he had a feeling it might be, to Joni. There were so many places where this could all go wrong and hurt them both. And that made him antsy.

He finished his mug of tea and kissed her lingeringly. 'I'd better let you get some sleep. Thanks for this evening.'

'No, thank *you*—you're the one who sorted it all out and it was fantastic.' She paused. 'Um, are you busy tomorrow?'

'Not particularly.'

'Give me a call if you fancy going for a walk or something. It might be nice to have a wander round Chelsea Physic Garden,' she said.

'That sounds good. I'll call you tomorrow.' He kissed her again. 'Goodnight, Nizhoni who most definitely lives up to her name.'

And her face turned a very gratifying shade of pink.

The weather the next morning was awful. So much for their planned walk around the medici-nal botanical garden at Chelsea, Aaron thought.

But he called Joni anyway. 'I've got waterproofs if you're game for walking round a garden in all this rain,' he said, 'but I guess we're not going to see that much.'

'I guess not,' she agreed. 'Unless we switch the venue to somewhere indoors. How about a wander around an art gallery or museum?'

'That works for me,' he said.

'Great. Where do you want to go?'

'I don't know London that well. Surprise me,' he suggested.

Half an hour later, he met her at her flat. Last night she'd been dressed to the nines; today, her face was scrubbed clean and she was wearing jeans and a T-shirt teamed with flat canvas shoes. But she was still utterly beautiful, and even looking at her made his heart skip a beat.

He kissed her hello. 'You're wearing your hair back.'

She shrugged. 'I can loosen it, if you want.'

'It's up to you how you wear your hair,' he said, remembering that her ex had been a control freak. 'But I think it's too gorgeous to hide in a ponytail.'

She blushed prettily and smiled. 'Thank you.' She took the scrunchie out of her hair and stuffed it into her pocket, then shook her hair loose. 'Are you ready to go?'

'Sure. Where are we going?'

'You told me to surprise you. I can't do that if I tell you where we're going,' she pointed out.

He laughed. 'You're just trying to get your own back for me doing the Man of Mystery stuff last night.'

She grinned. 'Just a little bit. Though you set the bar a bit on the high side. I need a bit of time to research somewhere different.'

'Or maybe we could make a list together,' he said.

Her smile warmed him all the way through. 'Now, that,' she said, 'is an excellent idea. We'll make a list of quirky stuff we want to do, together. Today we're going to somewhere that's pretty well known, but I still think it's worth a visit.'

'That works for me,' he said. Particularly because it meant he was spending time with her.

Walking in the rain with her to the tube station

was fun, because it meant being tucked under an umbrella together and it was a great excuse to put his arm round her.

Before Joni, Aaron had never really thought of himself as the tactile type. But he liked being close to her. Liked being able to smell her floral scent. Liked the warmth of her skin next to his hand. It made him feel as if he was in same kind of brave new world—one that was full of wonder and brightness. Joni made all his senses feel hyper-alert—and he was really starting to like that feeling.

They left the train at Charing Cross. Aaron still wasn't quite sure where she had in mind until they reached the church of St Martin in the Fields and she stopped and indicated a poster that was advertising a concert that afternoon. 'I love Bach.' Then she looked worried, as if she was being too demanding. Was that how her ex had made her feel? Her next words confirmed exactly what she was worrying about. 'Do you have time to go to that as well as where we're going now?'

He wanted to reassure her—but, at the same

time, he didn't want her to feel stifled or as if he was just humouring her. It was a fine line to walk, and he could still get it so very wrong. 'I have time and it's a great idea,' he said. 'Let's get the tickets now, so we don't have to worry about queuing later.'

Once they'd bought the tickets, she led him round the corner to Trafalgar Square and he recognised the building instantly. 'The National Gallery?'

'It's such a nice way to spend a Saturday morning,' she said. 'And I love their Van Goghs—it's the brightness and the light in the paintings.'

Aaron thoroughly enjoyed wandering around with her, hand in hand, looking at the paintings. After they'd grabbed a quick sandwich and a drink, Joni noticed that it had stopped raining. 'Let's go and see the lions,' she said. 'I know it's touristy, but I've always loved them. I've got a picture with me and the boys posing by the lions when we were really small, and it's one of my favourites.'

Family again.

Would she be able to cope with the fact that

his family wasn't close at all, or would it be a deal-breaker?

He pushed the thought away and walked round the fountain with her, then admired Nelson's Column.

'We have to do the touristy thing,' she said, and drew him over to one of the Landseer lions guarding the column. She held out her phone at arm's length to take a selfie of them with his arms wrapped round her and her cheek pressed against his; it made him feel as young and un-encumbered as the teenagers around them who were doing exactly the same thing. Which was weird, because he'd always been a serious and nerdy teen, throwing his energies into studying rather than partying.

And he enjoyed holding her hand all the way through the concert that afternoon: perfect music in a perfect environment and with perfect company,

Back at the tube station, he had a pretty good idea of how she'd felt when she'd asked him to go to the concert. Pretty much the way he was feeling now—worried that he was wanting too much, moving things too fast. But he asked anyway. 'I know I'm being greedy, but I'm not quite ready for today to end. Do you have time to have dinner with me?'

'I'd love to.' He realised that she actually had dimples when she smiled, dimples that made him want to sweep her off her feet, spin her round and kiss her until they were both dizzy, regardless of who could see them—and he'd never been that reckless.

Not good.

What had happened to his self-control? But he didn't have time to think about that when she added, 'And I know a very nice little Italian trattoria just round the corner.'

'That sounds perfect.'

And it was. Aaron really enjoyed talking to Joni about films and books, especially when he discovered that she liked the same kind of arthouse films that he did. He also found himself sharing much more information about himself than he normally would. Which should have made him feel wary; yet with her he could relax.

He kissed her goodbye on her doorstep.

'Do you want to come in for a drink or something?' she asked.

Or something, he thought. He wanted to carry her to her bed. Peel her clothes off, exceedingly slowly. Find out just where and how she liked being touched—by both his hands and his mouth—and then keep doing it until she cried out his name in release.

But this wasn't the deal.

'Better not.'

She looked wary, and he remembered what she'd said about always being the one to put in all the effort. He needed to explain and take that wariness out of her eyes. 'Not because I don't want to, but because I don't want to rush things.'

'You don't want to rush things.'

She still looked wary, so he knew he had to make a little more effort. Even though he wasn't used to spilling his guts like this, she needed to hear it. 'I had a fabulous time with you today.'

His reward was her smile. A heartfelt one. 'Me, too.' She stroked his face. 'I'll see you at work on Monday. And thank you for a lovely day.'

All the way home, Aaron was smiling. And

then he realised why. He was actually *happy*. He couldn't ever remember feeling this kind of lightness in his soul.

Joni had definitely changed his life for the better. Yet a part of him wondered could it really stay like this? Or was he hoping for too much—from himself, as well as from her?

CHAPTER TEN

MONDAY MORNING SAW Aaron and Joni both rostered to the walk-in clinic. In the staff kitchen they exchanged a glance that made Joni feel hot all over, but she knew this wasn't the place to do what she really wanted and kiss him until his eyes grew dark and desire slashed colour through his cheeks. It was still early days, and they'd agreed to keep this just between them. Right now, they were colleagues—and, as far as everyone else was concerned, *just* colleagues. She gave him a professional smile. 'Did you have a good weekend?' she asked.

'Very nice. You?' he replied.

'One of the nicest I've had in ages,' she said. 'A bit of culture, seeing friends and my family. It doesn't get any better than that.'

And the warmth in his eyes told her that he knew exactly what she was saying.

Joni's first case that morning was a man who'd been seriously grumpy with the receptionist and had almost fallen foul of the hospital's zero-tolerance policy. But Joni knew that sometimes feeling ill could make people act out of character, so she decided to give him the benefit of the doubt.

'What seems to be the problem, Mr Gillespie?' she asked.

'I couldn't get in to see my GP so I've been to the emergency department and they were rubbish. They wouldn't let me talk and they kept interrupting me.' He scowled. 'They told me it was a summer cold or mild flu and to go and see a pharmacist to get something over the counter. The stuff the pharmacist gave me hasn't touched my headache, and I'm hot all over, and now I've got a rash. My back aches and my legs hurt.' He glared at her. 'And I'm fed up with people not listening to me.'

Feeling really rough and as if nobody would listen to him or help him—no wonder he'd been grumpy. 'Well, I'm definitely listening,' she said.

'As you're feeling hot, would you mind if I took your temperature?'

'It's about time someone did,' he complained, but he let her check his temperature with the ear thermometer.

'Your temperature's definitely too high,' she said, 'and I can see that your eyes are red as well. Do they hurt?'

'They itch,' he said.

'OK. I can give you something for that. May I see the rash?'

He lifted his T-shirt to reveal a purpuric rash on his torso.

'Given that this is the walk-in clinic for tropical medicine and infectious diseases, I know you've probably already been asked this, so I'm sorry to repeat it and ask you again,' she said gently, 'but have you been abroad at all recently?'

'I went to France two weeks ago,' he said.

'OK.' Hardly tropical, but Mr Gillespie's symptoms were definitely starting to look like those of a notifiable disease.

'On the first day I was in a kayak,' he said, 'on a river. And I capsized. I swallowed a lot of water. I started feeling ill a few days later—I've been sick and I had the runs, so I'm sure it was something in the water I swallowed.'

'I think you're right,' she said. 'Given that you have that rash, your eyes are red and sore and you have a high temperature, plus the fact that you've swallowed water from a river, I think there's a strong possibility that you have leptospirosis.'

'I *knew* I was ill,' he said. 'I'm going to complain about that other lot.'

'To be fair,' she said gently, 'the symptoms in the early stages of leptospirosis are really similar to those of flu, so it's a tricky one to diagnose. When did you first notice the rash?'

'Yesterday,' he said.

'I need to take a blood sample from you to confirm my diagnosis,' she said, 'but I'm going to start you on a week's course of antibiotics. Have you ever had any kind of allergic reaction to antibiotics in the past—a rash, swelling or nausea?'

'No.'

'Good—then you can take them at home,' she said. 'Leptospirosis is a bacterium, and it can survive for several months in water or damp soil. You're most likely to come into contact with the bacteria in canals or rivers, so you were right about that river making you ill.'

'Can anyone catch it from me?' he asked.

'No. It's not spread from person to person. It's spread by water or soil containing the bacteria entering a cut in your skin, or through your mucous membranes—your eyes or your mouth. I'm afraid this bit isn't very nice—usually it's spread by infected rats excreting the bacteria in their urine.'

'Infected rat pee?' He gagged.

'Sorry,' she said, 'but they don't necessarily look ill when they're infected so you wouldn't know that the water was full of spirochaetes.'

'I wish I'd never gone on that sailing trip. It was my brother's idea. I only went because he said we'd go to some vineyards and chateaux.' He grimaced. 'And my brother's fine. He didn't capsize.'

'Rotten luck for you,' she said sympathetically. 'Would you mind me taking a blood sample now?'

'I hate needles,' Mr Gillespie grumbled, but he let her take the sample.

She wrote out a prescription. 'You can take this into any pharmacy, and I want you to start taking them now. The bad news is that you'll probably still feel rough for the next couple of days, but the good news is that you should feel a lot better within a week.'

'Huh,' he said, and grimaced.

'But,' she said, 'sometimes the symptoms of leptospirosis can develop into something a bit more serious. So if you start to feel more unwell than you do now, or your skin and the whites of your eyes turn yellow, or your ankles swell up or you don't pass as much urine as usual, then I want you to come straight in and we'll admit you because you'll need more treatment.' She printed out a patient information leaflet for him. 'This is so you don't have to try and remember everything I said. And if you find that the rash and your high temperature and headache go for a little while but come back again, then I want you straight back here, OK? Don't go to your family doctor or the emergency department—come straight here.'

'OK,' he said.

'I'll call you with the results of the blood test and let you know if I want you to come back and change your treatment, but these antibiotics should clear it up.'

'Thank you,' he said. 'And I'm never going sailing, *ever* again.'

'I don't blame you,' she said.

Joni was rushed off her feet for the rest of the morning, but she managed to meet Aaron for a snatched sandwich during their lunch break. 'How was your morning?'

'Full of gastro problems—things that probably aren't the right things to discuss at this moment,' he said, indicating their lunch. 'How was yours?'

'I had a case of leptospirosis.'

'Unusual,' he said. 'Local?'

'No. He capsized a kayak in a river in France,' she explained. 'The poor guy swallowed a lot of water.'

'And unless you'd been warned about the area,

you wouldn't necessarily know that there was leptospirosis around.'

'Not until you started getting the gastro problems, then the high temperature, the conjunctivitis and the rash appeared,' she agreed.

'Does he have jaundice?' he asked.

'Not right now, and I'm keeping my fingers crossed it doesn't develop that far.'

And how good it was to be able to sit with him and chat easily about work. Marty had always been bored by her work, though he'd been very happy to talk about his own. Aaron actually listened.

And life, Joni thought, was good. Really good.

That evening, as usual Joni met Bailey for their yoga class and dinner afterwards.

'You're glowing,' Bailey said when they'd sat down in the restaurant and had ordered their meal.

'We did a lot of downward dogs in class, so it must be all that blood rushing to my head,' Joni said.

Bailey grinned. 'Yeah, right. It wouldn't have

anything to do with a certain tropical medicine doctor who wears glasses, would it?'

Joni blushed.

'So you're dating officially?' Bailey asked. At Joni's nod, she said, 'Good. I think he might be just what you need after Marty the Maggot.'

'We're just seeing how it goes,' Joni said. 'He's coming to Olly's gig on Wednesday. But that's as part of the team, not as my date—we're keeping it just between us for now. So don't say anything to Mum and Dad, will you?'

'Of course not.' Bailey patted her hand. 'It's nice to see you looking happy.'

'I am.' Joni smiled. 'But we'll see how it goes.'

On the Wednesday evening. a group from the tropical medicine department went for a meal straight after work, and then headed to the pub where Joni's brother's band was playing.

Her family was already there and greeted her with a hug and kiss.

'Everyone, this is Aaron, our new consultant,' she said.

So she was introducing him to her family as

her colleague rather than her date. Aaron knew why she'd said it—it was still early days between them—but it still stung a bit.

He had to make an effort to follow the rest of her conversation.

'Aaron, these are my parents, Sam and Marianna Parker, and my brothers, Luke and Olly. Aaron's a blues fan, so that's why I dragged him out with us all tonight,' she explained.

'Olly's band is amazing,' Marianna said, and then she grinned. 'Not that I'm at *all* biased, as his mother.'

Aaron smiled. 'Joni said almost exactly the same thing. I'm looking forward to this.'

'She's already told me that we like the same kind of music—and that you've seen my favourite band four times,' Olly said, giving him a high five. 'I'm going to have to be boring and rush off now and set up stuff on stage, but I'll see you later, OK, and we'll catch up then?'

'Sure,' Aaron said.

'So how are you settling into London?' Sam asked.

'Fine, thanks—it's a great department and they're a good bunch of people to work with.'

'They certainly are,' Sam said.

'Where are you from?' Marianna asked.

'Manchester.'

'That's quite a way from here—do you have family in London at all?' she asked.

Yes, but that would open a can of worms. 'My family's a bit scattered around the globe,' he said. 'They're all in the armed forces, except me.' And he was the only one in four generations who'd turned his back on that way of life. It hadn't gone down well.

'You didn't want to be an army doctor?' Sam asked, unintentionally rubbing a sore spot.

'Battlefield medicine isn't for me. I wanted to do something a bit different,' Aaron said.

'And tropical medicine's such an interesting area,' Marianna said. 'Has Joni told you about her research proposal?'

'Yes, and it's fascinating,' Aaron said.

Marianna and Sam both looked pleased, and Luke talked to him about football and beer and his favourite buildings until the support act came on. Aaron could understand now why Joni was so warm. Her family was just like her—sweet and kind and making everyone feel included.

Joni's friend Bailey arrived just when the support act had finished and gave Joni a hug. 'Sorry I'm late. The game went on a bit and I had to strap up a knee. Hopefully my patient isn't going to end up with cartilage damage.'

Joni introduced them swiftly. 'Bailey, this is Aaron Hughes, our new consultant. Aaron, this is Bailey Randall, my best friend.'

'The sports medicine specialist and endorphin fiend, right?' he said with a smile, shaking Bailey's hand.

Bailey smiled back at him and he knew that she recognised him; he also had the strongest feeling that she knew exactly what was happening between him and Joni, but she wasn't going to blow their cover.

He chatted to her until Olly's band came on.

He enjoyed the gig, but there was one blues song in particular where he really wanted to wrap his arms round Joni and hold her close. He knew he couldn't do that or it would make things awkward for her; but he was disappointed that he didn't even get the chance to walk her home and kiss her goodnight on her doorstep.

Aaron managed to have a quick coffee with her between clinics the next day, on the pretext of talking through a case.

'I enjoyed the gig last night,' he said. 'Your brother's very talented.'

She looked proud. 'Yes, he is.'

'I noticed you introduced me to your family as your colleague.'

She spread her hands. 'Aaron, half of the department was with us and we agreed this is just between us for now. If I'd told Mum and Dad we were seeing each other, someone would've overheard us and we'd be the hottest topic on the hospital grapevine right now.'

'Fair point,' he said. It wasn't nice to think that everyone was talking about you.

'Plus,' she added, 'if I'd told my family who you really are, they would've grilled you, and I'm not sure you're ready for that.'

'Probably not,' he agreed. 'Sorry, I shouldn't have called you on it.'

'It's OK—though, actually, it's nice that you minded,' she said. 'Just so you know, I minded, too.'

'Bailey knows, though?' he asked.

She wrinkled her nose. 'Bailey's my best friend—as close as if she were my sister. She's not going to tell anyone.'

'Thank you,' he said quietly. And he was glad she had someone fighting her corner for her. 'What do you want to do at the weekend?'

'I was thinking,' she said, 'it might be fun to see the pelicans being fed in St James's Park on Saturday afternoon. Dad used to take me there when I was tiny and I always loved it.'

'Sounds good to me. Let me know where and when you want me to meet you.' He finished his coffee. 'I've got clinic. I'd better run. Catch you later.'

He thought about her family's warmth all the way home. Maybe if he made a bit more effort, his own family could be like that. Then again, it had never been their style. He was expecting too much from them, and that wasn't fair.

And it also gave Aaron pause for thought. He

couldn't offer Joni anything near what she could offer him. His family would be distant with her and he knew it would hurt her. Given that her own family was so close, he didn't have a clue how to explain it to her. How could she possibly understand their stiff upper lip stance when she'd never grown up with it? So maybe he ought to back off a little and give her the space to cool things down between them.

The only problem was, he didn't want to.

But maybe he ought to stop being selfish and put her needs before his own.

On Friday morning, a worried-looking couple walked in with a letter of referral from their family doctor.

'Pete thinks it's a summer virus and I'm making a fuss over nothing,' Mrs Kirby said, 'but I've got a bad feeling about this.'

And so did the GP, from the look of the referral. *Suspected EBLV from bat bite.*

European Bat Lyssavirus—also known as bat rabies —was a rabies-like virus transmitted by bats, which could kill if symptoms developed.

And there was nothing in the letter about any rabies vaccination being administered. Classic rabies, transmitted by dogs, cats and other animals, was almost unknown in the UK. Joni had dealt with a couple of precautionary cases when a local zookeeper had been bitten or scratched by an imported exotic animal with suspected rabies, but all the zookeepers had been vaccinated against rabies, and all of them had come in as soon as they'd been infected and well before any symptoms had started. The usual procedure—cleaning the wound thoroughly and administering vaccination post-exposure to stop the infection spreading—had worked.

But a case where symptoms had already started…Joni knew exactly why Mrs Kirby was panicking. She'd be panicking, too, in the other woman's shoes because, once the patient started having symptoms, bat rabies could be fatal and the only treatment you could give was to sedate the patient and keep them comfortable until they fell into a coma and died from heart failure.

'Would you like to tell me about your symptoms and a bit of the background as to what happened?' Joni asked gently.

Mr Kirby grimaced. 'I'm an art restorer and I conserve wall paintings. I was working in a church—there are bats in the tower, but normally they don't bother me when I'm working. Something must've spooked them last week, because they all rushed out past me in a flock. I was up a ladder at the time and it caught me by surprise, and I banged my hand. I didn't feel as if I'd been bitten—if anything, I probably just caught my hand on a nail or something—but Debs here reckons I was bitten, because I've been feeling a bit off for the last couple of days.'

'He's got a sore throat, a headache and a high temperature, but he's shivering and says he feels chilly,' Mrs Kirby said.

'It's just a summer flu,' her husband said. 'There's a nasty bug doing the rounds.'

'But you've been irritable. You're not normally like that. And you said your hand was tingling.'

'Probably an allergic reaction to something I've been using in the church. You spill stuff and it gets on your skin,' he said, flapping a dismis-sive hand.

'But bats can spread rabies, or something that's like it,' Mrs Kirby said, looking anxious.

'European Bat Lyssavirus,' Joni confirmed. 'It's often called bat rabies.'

'Supposing one of them did bite you and you just didn't feel it?' Mrs Kirby asked.

'We can do some blood tests to check,' Joni said, 'and test your saliva as well. If there are EBLV antibodies, then we know what we're dealing with.'

'And you can treat it?' Mrs Kirby asked.

Not if it developed into full-blown bat rabies. And the sad thing was that if he'd come into the department on the day he'd been bitten, even though he hadn't had any previous vaccinations against rabies, the immunoglobulin and post-exposure vaccine would've been enough to deal with the virus. 'I'll be able to tell you more when I see the results of the blood tests,' Joni said, not wanting to worry the Kirbys further. 'Mr Kirby, can I ask you, did you notice any unusual be-haviour among the bats?'

'They were just a bit spooked. There were a lot of them and they rushed about in the church for a few minutes. The poor verger had a hell of a job cleaning up when they finally went back to their roost. There was guano everywhere.' He shrugged. 'I can't really tell you anything more than that.'

'OK.' Now for the hard questions. The ones she didn't want to worry them with, but she needed to know the answers. 'Have you had any difficulty swallowing, or sweated more than normal, or have you felt unusually anxious?'

'No. Debs is worrying about nothing,' Mr Kirby insisted, but he allowed Joni to take blood and saliva samples.

Once she'd taken the samples and sent them to the lab, she went in search of Aaron. 'I need to pick your brains. Have you come across many cases of EBLV?'

'It's pretty rare, though I've had two or three back in Manchester,' Aaron said. 'A couple were zookeepers who got bitten, and one was a bat handler. Luckily they'd all had vaccinations and they all came in pretty much as soon as they'd been bitten, so I could treat them promptly enough to avoid them developing the full-blown virus.' He raised an eyebrow. 'Is that what you've had this morning? A zookeeper who's been bitten?'

'No, my patient's a restoration specialist—but he was working in a church and he *might* have been bitten by a bat. Before you ask, no, he hasn't ever been vaccinated.'

'Clean the wound with hydrogen peroxide, give him rabies immunoglobulin and start him on a course of the rabies vaccine,' Aaron advised. 'That should stop the virus developing.'

'There's one teensy, teensy problem,' Joni said. 'It happened a week ago, and he isn't sure if he was bitten—he says the bats were spooked and came round him in a flock, and he banged his hand. He thinks he's just got summer flu, and the symptoms he describes are the same as flu.'

Aaron grimaced. 'And as early bat rabies.'

She nodded. 'His wife is convinced he was bitten, and his GP's clearly working on the safe side and referred him to us.'

'Have you taken bloods?' Aaron asked.

'And saliva samples. I've sent everything off to the lab.' She bit her lip. 'But if the results show he has the antibodies as well as the early symptoms, there's nothing we can do, is there?'

'All we'll be able to do for him then is to give him sedatives, to protect him from the pain and the emotional upset.' Aaron looked thoughtful. 'Though there is maybe something. My boss in Manchester went to a conference a couple of years back and there was a session about the Milwaukee protocol.'

'A cure?' she asked.

'It's pretty experimental and has a very low success rate,' he warned. 'They think it might not actually be the treatment that makes the patient survive—instead, it might be because of something in their immune systems, or they were infected with a weak strain of the virus.'

'But it's worked on some people?' At his nod, Joni continued, 'Then it's better than the alternative—which is doing nothing and just letting him die.' She blew out a breath. 'I'm getting ahead of myself. I'll wait and see what the tests show before I start panicking. But, if it's bat rabies, can I come and grab you?'

'Of course. Unless you'd rather ask Mr Flinders, because he might have more experience in the area.'

She shook her head. 'I'm happy to take advice from you. You're a consultant—even if you are barely out of nappies.'

He rolled his eyes at her. 'Hardly. I'm three years older than you are.'

'And you're still the youngest consultant I know. To get this far, this soon, you're seriously good at your job. Plus you have more experience than I do.'

'Well, thanks for the compliment,' he said, sounding a little awkward and yet a little pleased at the same time. 'Come and get me if you need me.'

Aaron was writing up some notes later that afternoon when Joni rapped on his door.

'You got the tests back?' he asked.

'Yup. Just now.' She blew out a breath. 'It's not good news. It's definitely bat rabies.'

'Right. You need to talk to your patient.'

'And his wife.'

'I'll come with you. We'll have to tell them what the options are and see what they want us to do,' Aaron said. 'I can't promise the Milwaukee protocol will work.'

'But at least it gives them a chance,' Joni said softly. 'Which is better than nothing. I'd take it—wouldn't you?'

A few months ago, Aaron wouldn't have been that fussed either way. He did his job—and that was who and what he was. But since Joni had come into his life… 'Yes. Let's go and see them.'

Joni introduced Aaron to the Kirbys.

'It's bad news, isn't it?' Mrs Kirby asked. 'Otherwise you wouldn't have brought another doctor in with you.'

'I'm sorry,' Joni said. 'The test results show you were infected by one of the bats.'

'So I have bat rabies?' Mr Kirby asked.

She nodded.

'And there isn't a cure for it,' Mrs Kirby said.

'I'm so sorry,' Joni said again.

'So I'm going to die?' Mr Kirby looked

shocked. 'Oh, my God. I'm going to run around, foaming at the mouth and being afraid of water and biting people?'

'It's not a fear of water and you won't bite anyone. Though you will produce a lot more saliva,' Joni said, 'and you'll find it harder and harder to swallow.'

He shook his head. 'I can't take it in.'

'There is an alternative,' Aaron said. 'I need to tell you that we can't guarantee it will definitely work. It's an experimental treatment with a low success rate so far.'

'But at least it gives me a chance of surviving,' Mr Kirby said. 'From what you've just said, it's my only chance, so I'll take it. What do you have to do?'

'We think that the way the rabies virus works is that it affects your brain before your body can fight the infection,' Aaron explained. 'So if we put you into a medically induced coma to protect your brain, we can give you antiviral medication to help your body fight the disease.'

'A bit like that bloke who had the skiing accident and hit his head—they kept him in a coma until they'd treated him, didn't they?' Mr Kirby asked.

'A bit like that, yes,' Aaron said. 'We can give you fluids and electrolytes on a drip, so we can keep your body functioning—and you won't know anything about it.'

'And if it doesn't work, then I don't get the thing where I can't swallow,' Mr Kirby said.

'We wouldn't let you go through that anyway,' Joni said. 'If you'd rather not give this a try—and as my senior colleague said, it *is* an experimental procedure and it might not work—then we'd give you some medication to keep you comfortable and also so you wouldn't be aware of what was happening to you.'

Mr Kirby looked at his wife. 'So it's die, or give it a go and it probably won't work, but there's a tiny outside chance it might and I'll be back to normal.'

'If it does work, there might still be some damage from the virus and you might need some rehab before you get back to normal,' Aaron said. 'But you've summed it up pretty well.'

Mr Kirby blew out a breath. 'OK. I'll do it. But

I want to see the kids first. I want to say good-bye to them, just in case it doesn't work.'

'We can arrange that. And if there's anything either of you need, anything at all, you just ask,' Joni said.

Saying goodbye to the kids.

Aaron hadn't really had the chance to say goodbye to Ned. His brother had been in a coma because of the malaria. And, even though doctors thought that patients in a coma might be able to hear, Aaron would never know if Ned had heard his last words. Saying that he loved him, he was going to be a doctor like Ned planned to be, and he'd make his brother proud of him. Do his best to save people, the way the doctors hadn't been able to save Ned.

And he'd kept his promise. He'd worked hard, and he'd saved most of his patients. He might not be able to do that for Mr Kirby, but he'd try his very hardest. And by his side there would be the one person he was beginning to realise he could rely on—Joni. Working with him. Keeping him going through the tough times with the sweetness of her smile.

Under the table, he reached for her hand and squeezed it.

As if she guessed what he was thinking, she returned the pressure.

They'd do their best. Together.

On Saturday afternoon, Joni and Aaron walked hand in hand through St James's Park to find the rock on the lake where the pelicans were spreading their wings and basking in the sun. The second that the wildlife officer appeared by the lake with his bucket of fish, they came over and crowded around him, eager to be fed— just as the children in the park crowded around, eager to see.

'The pelicans have been here in the park since 1664, when the very first one was a gift from the Russian Ambassador,' the wildlife officer explained. 'They eat the fish in the lake, but they also like the mackerel and herring I bring them.' He tossed a fish to each bird, which caught it deftly. 'We did have a pelican who used to fly over to London Zoo and steal their fish for his lunch, but these ones are all happy to wait for me to turn up.'

Joni enjoyed the show, but she noticed that Aaron had gone quiet. Maybe seeing the pelicans wasn't his kind of thing; after all, they hadn't got round to doing their list of places they wanted to go and see together.

But as the afternoon went on he became quieter and quieter, and she knew she was going to have to broach the subject because she hated this awkwardness between them.

'Aaron, is something wrong?' she asked.

'No.'

His expression was absolutely unreadable. It was obvious to her that something was wrong, but she didn't have a clue what it was. Or maybe he was seeing what Marty saw in her, so this relationship was going to be just as much of a failure as her broken engagement—and it was all her fault for not being good enough.

'I'm sorry,' she said miserably.

He frowned. 'What for?'

'Obviously I've said something wrong.' She spread her hands. 'Or done something wrong.

Or not done or said something that I should've done or said.'

'No, of course you haven't.' His frown deepened. 'Joni, why are you apologising to me?'

'I…' She didn't want to explain that.

'Is this what used to happen with Marty?' he asked.

Yes. Way too often.

She couldn't bring herself to answer, too ashamed to admit the truth, and looked away.

Gently, he cupped her face. 'Look at me, Joni,' he said softly.

Warily, not sure what she'd see in his expression, she did so.

'You've done nothing wrong. *Nothing*,' he emphasised.

'I just…' How could she explain?

He kissed the tip of her nose. 'It's not you. It's me. I'm sorry. It's stupid stuff in my head—and I promise you it's nothing to do with you.' He sighed. 'I did warn you I'm not very good at relationships. But promise me you'll never apologise to me again.'

'I'm sor—' she began, and stopped herself. She grimaced. 'Um.'

He smiled. 'I think that one was fineable—and I bet Bailey would agree with me if I asked her.'

The tightness between her shoulders eased. 'You're going to fine me for using the s-word?'

'Yup. I was thinking about making you buy me an ice cream as a fine, but I've just had a better idea—instead, it means you have to have dinner with me tonight. I'll cook for us.' He paused. 'If you're not busy, that is. Otherwise we can do it some other time.'

No, she wasn't busy. 'Does that mean I get fabulous coffee from your flashy machine?' she asked, not wanting to appear *too* available.

'It might do. If you ask me very nicely,' he teased.

Relief flooded through her. This was going to be all right.

She stood on tiptoe. 'Pretty please with sugar on it?' She kissed him lightly on the lips.

He wrapped his arms around her. 'That'll do very nicely.'

Back at Aaron's flat, she noticed all kinds of

things that she hadn't had time to notice on the night of the salsa club. She hadn't seen his living room before; it was all very neat, but there was only one shelf of medical textbooks, and there were no films or music or fiction.

'I thought you liked music,' she said.

'I do.'

'But you don't have any.'

He smiled. 'It's all digital. The same with my films—I stream them. It saves all the clutter.'

'And your books?'

'Also digital,' he said, 'apart from those medical textbooks. Weirdly, I prefer the old-fashioned way when it comes to work.'

There were no family photographs, either, and nothing personal that really told her anything about who he was. Maybe he'd learned to live in such a pared-down world because he'd had to pack up everything very quickly, either to move on to a new posting with his family in the army, or to move between their home and boarding school at either end of term. Though she wasn't going to ask him, because she didn't want to make him feel uncomfortable.

She followed him into the kitchen, where he was rummaging in his fridge.

'Is there anything I can do to help?' she asked.

'No, just sit and chat to me,' he said, and made her a frothy cappuccino just the way she liked it.

'This is fabulous,' she said. 'I feel very spoiled.'

He kissed her lightly. 'Good. That's my intention—and hopefully the spinach and chicken risotto will be a little bit better than a bacon sandwich.'

She grinned. 'I'll have you know that bacon sandwich was awesome. The only thing missing was avocado.'

'So that's your weakness?'

'One of them.' She noticed he wasn't using a recipe book. 'So this is one of your staples?'

He shrugged. 'It's a fairly basic recipe. I just tweak it depending on my mood.'

Marty had never cooked for Joni. He'd always expected her to do the cooking—and she'd been spineless enough to let him get away with it, instead of pointing out that her job was just as demanding as his and asking him to do his share of the chores.

'Thanks,' she said. 'Just so you know, I really appreciate it.'

'Good.' He stole a kiss, then went back to cooking for them.

After dinner, they watched a film in his living room, curled up on his sofa together. Wrapped in his arms, Joni felt warm and safe, and happier than she'd felt in a very long time.

As if he could guess at her thoughts, Aaron drew her just that little bit closer. He pushed her hair over one shoulder, and she felt his mouth against the nape of her neck—soft, sweet, enticing kisses. She closed her eyes and tipped her head to one side, giving him better access, and his lips grazed the side of her neck, finding the sensitive spot that made her quiver.

His hands slid beneath the hem of her T-shirt and he splayed his fingers over her midriff.

'Aaron,' she murmured, and shifted in his arms to face him.

He took full advantage of her new position and kissed her, his lips teasing and coaxing hers into a response. In turn, she untucked his shirt and slid her hands under the material, running her fingers across the hard wall of his abdomen. 'You feel so good,' she whispered.

He let his hands slide further up under her T-shirt, unclipping her bra and then cupping her breasts in his hands. 'So do you,' he said hoarsely. 'So soft. I need to see you, Joni.'

She kissed him. 'Yes.'

It didn't take him long to remove her T-shirt.

She coughed. 'Equals, remember.'

He laughed, and stripped off his own shirt. 'As you wish.'

Catching the movie reference, she laughed back, and let her fingers stray over his pectoral muscles. 'For a geek, you're in amazing shape. I love just looking at you,' she said.

He stole a kiss. 'Looking isn't enough for me right now.'

'Then touch me. Kiss me,' she said, and closed her eyes, and he kissed a path down her throat, meandering across her collarbones to linger in the hollows for a moment, then nuzzled his way down her sternum and took one nipple into his mouth.

'That's so good,' she whispered.

'Yes.' His voice was husky with need. 'Have I told you how gorgeous you are?'

'Keep talking,' she invited.

And then she wished she'd kept her mouth shut when he stopped touching her and pulled back.

'This was meant to be taking things slowly,' he said. 'Getting to know each other.'

She felt the colour staining her face. 'And I'm acting like a tart.'

'No.' He leaned over to kiss her lightly. 'Just I find you very hard to resist. It's never been like this for me. I've always been in control. But, with you, it's different.'

'Different good or different bad?' The words slipped out, needy and embarrassing, before she could stop them. Annoyed with herself, she crossed her arms across her breasts. 'You don't have to answer that.'

'Yes, I do. Definitely different good. Scary,' he said, 'but good.' He laid one palm against her cheek. 'Joni. Much as I'd like to carry you to my bed right now and spend the rest of the night making love with you, I'm not going to.'

Because she wasn't enough? Just as she hadn't been enough for Marty?

Either it showed in her face or he knew her well enough to guess what she was thinking, because he said softly, 'I don't want to rush this or take you for granted. I want to cherish you.' He kissed her. 'We have all the time in the world, and I want this to be a proper courtship.'

From Aaron, that was tantamount to a declaration of intent. She sat up and kissed him back. 'That's the sweetest thing anyone's ever said to me.'

'It comes from the heart.' He took her hand and placed it over his heart. She could feel how strong his heartbeat was, how fast. And all for her.

'From the heart,' she echoed. 'Then, if you wouldn't mind turning your back or closing your eyes, I'll get dressed again.'

He smiled. 'This time, Nizhoni who lives up to her name, I will. Next time...'

And the very idea of what he was implying sent a thrill all the way through her.

CHAPTER ELEVEN

OVER THE NEXT couple of weeks, Joni was really happy. She was in tune with Aaron at work, and she felt they were getting closer as they continued dating. They had similar tastes, and they'd enjoyed compiling a list together of all the quirky places they really wanted to visit. Best of all, Joni felt that both of them were losing the fear that this thing between them was all going to go pear-shaped. She still knew next to nothing about his family and he hadn't suggested meeting hers again, but she was sure that all they needed was a little time.

And, incredibly, they'd managed to pull off the one thing they hadn't quite dared to hope for. Mr Kirby, their patient with bat rabies, had been in a coma for ten days—long enough for the antiviral medication and the immunoglobulin to work. They'd brought him out of his coma very gradually, but it seemed that the virus had been the weaker strain often found in bats, or the experimental treatment really did work because he'd actually survived his ordeal. There was some damage to his speech and motor systems, but she knew that rehab would help with that.

'And it's all thanks to you,' she said to Aaron when they'd managed to sneak off to lunch.

He shrugged it off. 'I just knew about the treatment. You're the one who put everything into place.'

'Then it's down to great teamwork,' she said, giving him her sunniest smile.

'I'll drink to that,' Aaron said, raising his mug of coffee. 'So how was your morning?'

'Mostly OK, apart from my poor man from the other week with leptospirosis—he came back in today and I had to admit him.'

'He's developed jaundice?' Aaron guessed.

She nodded. 'I think he might need dialysis in the next couple of days.'

'Even if he does, the damage to his kidneys should repair itself over the next couple of months,' Aaron said.

'That's what I told him, though the poor man's worried sick.'

'If you want me to come and support you next time you talk to him, give me a yell,' he said.

She smiled at him. 'Thanks. I might just take you up on that. Not because I doubt my diagnosis, but I think Mr Gillespie could just do with a bit of extra reassurance, and you're senior to me.'

'Your skills are as good as mine,' Aaron said, 'but I know what you mean about a patient's point of view. Consider it done.'

On Saturday morning, they met at Joni's flat. 'I thought we could do something really foodie today,' she told Aaron. 'How do you fancy going to one of the oldest markets in London, right next to London Bridge?'

'Sounds good to me,' he said.

They caught the tube to Borough Market and spent an hour browsing through the stalls. Joni was pleased to discover a stall selling granola suitable for diabetics, and Aaron was thrilled to discover a coffee stall selling some of the blends he'd bought back in Manchester. He ended up having a very geeky conversation with the barista about brewing coffee, much to Joni's amusement.

'So you're telling me that there are floral notes in coffee?' she asked.

'There is in this one. And I'll prove it,' Aaron said and ordered them both a cappuccino without chocolate on the top.

It was a much lighter roast than Joni was used to, but she could see what he meant. 'It's nice,' she said.

'Good. I'm glad you like it.' Aaron bought two bags of beans. 'So how far are we from St Paul's?' he asked.

'You want to have a look round the cathedral and do the Whispering Gallery?' she asked.

'No. There's a park on our list that's nearby. It has a really interesting memorial.'

'I know the one you mean,' she said. 'It's not that far. We could take the tube—or, as it's a nice day, we could just walk over the bridge. You can see St Paul's from here on the other side of the river. It's less than half an hour's walk.'

'So we could have a picnic in the park,' he suggested.

'Great idea.'

They bought artisan bread, ham, tomatoes and artisan cheese for lunch, along with a punnet of peaches and some bottles of water, then walked over the bridge, hand in hand. It took them a little while to find the park, and the space was almost empty when they walked in, apart from a scattering of pigeons.

'That's it,' he said, gesturing to a wall with a tiled roof above it to protect it from the weather. 'The Watts Memorial to Heroic Self Sacrifice— named after the Victorian painter who set it up. He wanted to tell the stories of ordinary people who died saving others. Apparently it was meant to be for Queen Victoria's Golden Jubilee, but the committee rejected the idea. He eventually set it up with the vicar of the nearby church. After his death, his widow continued the gallery for a while, but then she was busy with other things and it was abandoned halfway through.'

They went over to take a closer look.

'Dr Alexander Stewart Brown,' she read.

'"Though suffering from severe spinal injury the result of a recent accident died from his brave efforts to rescue a drowning man and to restore his life." I wonder what happened?'

'I did find a website with more information about the stories behind the plaques. Hang on.' Aaron looked it up on his phone. 'Apparently he was convalescing in Boulogne after a carriage accident that damaged his back. He was walking on the pier when he saw a man drowning in the sea. He jumped in to rescue the man, worked on him for two hours and saved his life—but ended up catching a bad cold, which turned to pneumonia.'

'Poor man,' Joni said. 'And this one's tragic— "George Lee, fireman. At a fire in Clerkenwell carried an unconscious girl to the escape falling six times and died of his injuries."'

'And this one,' he said. '"Samuel Rabbeth, medical officer of the Royal Free Hospital, who tried to save a child suffering from diphtheria at the cost of his own life."' He looked it up. 'The little boy was only four. They gave him a tracheotomy, but a membrane was still obstructing his breathing. Rabbeth put a tube in and tried to suck the membrane out—and he ended up getting diphtheria himself.'

They looked at each other. 'Nowadays we have a lot more protection,' she said, 'with barrier nursing and prophylactic medicine and what have you—but I guess we'd still take risks if we thought we could save someone and it was the only way.' She shivered. 'It's kind of nice that these people have been commemorated—saving people from drowning and fires and the like—but how sad.'

Aaron held her close. 'Sorry. I didn't mean to make you unhappy.'

'Not unhappy, exactly—just realising how lucky we are,' she said. 'I guess you need to enjoy every moment of life, because you never know what's just round the corner.'

'"Gather ye rosebuds while ye may."' He kissed her lightly. 'Come on. Let's have our picnic and enjoy the sunshine.'

Just being with him made her feel relaxed and happy, and she enjoyed sharing the food they'd bought from the deli stalls.

'I was going to ask you,' he said, 'what traditional Diné food was like.'

And he'd used the right term, she thought with a smile. He'd paid attention. He was interested in her heritage and respected it. And it felt so good to be accepted for who she was—to feel as if she was *enough*. 'It's fairly simple stuff—bread, vegetables, meat and fish. The Diné are basically farmers,' she said. 'I could cook something traditional for you tonight, if you like. We'll need to go to the supermarket on the way home to pick up a couple of things.'

'Sounds good to me,' he said. 'I'd really like that. If I'm not imposing.'

She laughed. ''Course you're not. And you can help with the washing up. I'm not proud.'

He laughed back. 'You're on.'

Joni was as comfortable with him sitting in her kitchen while she cooked as he seemed to be with her. 'So this is Navajo stew—sweet potatoes, bell peppers and onions. You just roast the lot in the oven, add it to a tomato and dried smoked chilli sauce along with black beans, let it bubble for a bit, and serve it with grilled fish.' She smiled. 'And fried bread. I love it when *shimá sání* makes this. It's a real treat.'

'Fried bread?'

'It isn't quite as artery-clogging as it sounds,' she said with a grin. 'It's a bit like an Indian paratha—you make bread, roll it out until it's really thin like a French pancake, and then fry it on both sides.'

'This is fantastic,' Aaron said when she'd finished cooking dinner and he'd set the table.

'It's very simple, but it's a good combination of flavours,' she said with a smile.

Afterwards, they curled up on her sofa together.

'I haven't been this happy in a long while,' he said softly. 'You've made my world a brighter place.'

Her eyes filled with tears.

'Joni? Why are you crying?'

'That's just such a nice thing to say.' She swallowed hard. 'Sorry, I'm being wet.'

'No, you're not.' He kissed away the single tear that had spilled over her lashes.

'You've made my world a brighter place, too,' she said softly.

'I'm glad. I like you, Joni. I like you a lot.'

'I like you a lot, too.' More than a lot, but she wasn't quite ready to voice it. 'Stay tonight?' she asked softly. 'I can't promise you good coffee, but I can promise you the best bacon sandwich for breakfast.'

He kissed her. 'Are you sure about this?'

She nodded. 'Slowly isn't enough for me any more.'

'Me neither.' He looked at her. 'So what do you want, Joni?'

'You,' she said simply. 'In my bed. Naked.' She paused. 'Inside me.'

It was as if she'd flipped a switch, because his eyes widened, and he scooped her up in his arms. 'Where's your bedroom?' His voice had dropped an octave; clearly he was picturing exactly what she'd just suggested, and he liked the idea as much as she did.

'Down the corridor, second on the right,' she said, and thoroughly enjoyed the fact that Aaron had turned into a caveman.

He set her down gently on her feet, pulled the curtains and switched the bedside light on. 'Are you sure about this?' he asked.

'Very sure,' she said.

He drew the hem of her T-shirt slowly upwards, and excitement began to fizz through her veins. They were going to be skin to skin again. At last. And this time he wasn't going to stop. She lifted her arms so he could pull her T-shirt over her head. And then he held her at arm's length, just looking at her.

'You're beautiful,' he said softly. 'So beautiful that you drive me out of my mind.'

That made two of them.

He drew one finger along the lacy edge of her bra. 'I like this,' he said. And then he unsnapped it and let the garment fall to the floor. 'But I like this even more.' His eyes were dark and intense as he cupped her breasts, rubbing the pad of his thumb across her hardened nipples.

'So do I,' she whispered. 'But I need more.'

'Good.' He gave her another of those intense looks, then dropped to his knees in front of her, took one nipple into his mouth and sucked. She slid her fingers into his hair, urging him on.

His hands stroked down over her back, curved over her bottom. Her jeans were in the way, and she wriggled against him in frustration. 'More,' she said.

He rocked back then, and gave her an insolent grin. 'More?'

'I need to be naked with you. Right now.'

He inclined his head, and undid the button of her jeans. She dragged in a breath; he was taking his sweet time about this, and it was exquisite torture.

At last, he lowered the zip. Eased the denim over her hips and peeled it down her legs. Slow, slow, slow.

She wriggled again. 'You're driving me crazy.'

'Good,' he said, with another of those insolent grins, and refused to hurry.

She whimpered. 'Aaron.'

'Slow and easy,' he said, completely inexorable.

She'd go insane if he kept this up.

But he still took it slowly, and her desire stoked

higher and higher as he took his time undressing her, stroking every bit of skin he uncovered, teasing her with his mouth.

Definitely insane, she thought. 'Aaron. Please.' She was begging now. She couldn't help herself. 'Touch me.'

'Here?' He stroked the hollows of her ankles.

'North,' she said.

'North.' He paused, as if pondering, and stroked the backs of her knees.

Since when had the backs of her knees been an erogenous zone? Knees weren't sexy. At all. And yet her temperature was climbing and she was wet, so wet and ready for him.

'More north,' she whispered.

'More north.' He paused again, and she quivered in anticipation of his next move. Which was to kiss her inner thigh.

'Warmer,' she said.

'Warmer. Hmm.'

She closed her eyes, knowing what he was going to do next, and wanting it so badly. And then she opened her eyes again in disbelief as he rubbed his cheek against her midriff.

'North, you said.'

'Too far.' And she actually whimpered, to her shame.

And then, at last, he slid his hand between her thighs. 'Warmer?' he asked with a grin.

As if he didn't know. And she was going to kill him if he teased her much more.

But then his thumb circled her clitoris.

'Better?' he asked softly.

'Almost.'

He did it again. And again. Until her body hit climax and her knees buckled.

But he was there to hold her, to support her until she could stand again. And then he scooped her up, laid her on the bed, and stripped in five seconds flat.

'What you said earlier,' he said. 'Naked. In your bed. And inside you.'

'Yes,' she said. 'Now.'

He paused for just long enough to slide on a condom, and then at last he knelt between her thighs and eased into her.

'Much better,' she said in satisfaction, and kissed him.

* * *

Much better, Aaron thought. He felt complete, here with her. Losing himself in her—and yet finding himself, too. With Joni, he was different. With Joni, he could be himself and the past didn't matter. And maybe, just maybe, he could do this. Do the emotional stuff. Connect with her in heart as well as in body.

She wrapped her legs round him, pulling him deeper, and he stopped thinking. All he could do was feel. The joy. The way his climax shattered through him—and made him feel reforged, stronger than before. Looking into her eyes, Aaron thought, I could love this woman. Really, really love her. Heart and soul.

Strangely, it didn't scare him. It simply made everything come into focus. Feel *real*.

And, when Joni fell asleep in his arms, Aaron felt more at peace than he had in years.

CHAPTER TWELVE

ON TUESDAY, A fifteen-year-old boy came in to the walk-in clinic with his mother.

'He went to Dominica with the school a month ago,' she told them. 'He said he took the malaria tablets while he was there. But I'm not sure you remembered all the time, Nick.'

'I did, Mum,' the boy protested. 'I didn't miss a dose. The teachers were really strict about it.'

Malaria. The disease that had coloured Aaron's whole life. He forced himself to lock the emotions away, the way he usually did, and schooled his voice to be as professional as possible. 'And you think he has malaria?' Aaron asked.

'He's got a headache and fever, he's shivering and he's had the runs,' Nick's mother said, 'though he hasn't thrown up. But if he took the tablets and they used mosquito nets and sprays, he can't have malaria, can he?'

'The tablets aren't always a hundred per cent effective,' Joni said.

Aaron was aware of her looking at him, her expression slightly anxious. Clearly she was worried that the case would upset him. But he was a doctor. His patients came first and his emotions came last. This was about treating the boy, not what had happened to Ned.

'And if you have been taking the tablets and you get malaria, then the symptoms show up later than if you haven't taken any of the tablets,' Aaron added.

'Can we examine you, please, Nick?' Joni asked.

Nick nodded, and let them check his pulse, blood pressure and sats.

'We're going to take a blood sample to confirm our suspicions,' Aaron said, 'and we should have the results back in about an hour, if you want to go and get a drink and something to eat in the meantime.'

The test came back positive for malaria.

'I'm sorry to say that you're right—you do have malaria, Nick,' Joni said. 'It's caused by the parasite *Plasmodium* and you get it through the bite of an infected mosquito—it can't be passed on by humans, so you don't have to worry that anyone else in the family will get it.'

Nick's mother looked worried. 'So how does he get treated? Do I have to give him tablets?'

'Actually, we're going to need to admit him to the ward,' Aaron said. 'The type of malaria Nick has is *Plasmodium falciparum,* which is the most serious one—we want you here so we can keep an eye on you, because sometimes you can get very ill very quickly with this type.'

Which was exactly what had happened to Ned. The parasite had destroyed his red blood cells, giving him severe anaemia. From there the infection had progressed to cerebral malaria, blocking the blood vessels to Ned's brain and finally killing him.

'The good news is that you're not showing any signs of complication at the moment,' Joni added.

'Your blood sugar is fine and the parasite count is less than two per cent, which is good—and if we do see a single sign of anything changing, we'll be able to treat it for you straight away,' Aaron explained. 'We're going to give you antimalarial medication, which will kill off the parasite, and I'm afraid you're going to get quite used to needles because we'll need to do a blood test every day to check the parasite count.'

'But try not to worry,' Joni said, 'because we'll keep a very close eye on you and you should get better, though you might feel rough for a few days yet.'

At the end of the clinic, after they'd admitted the boy to the ward, Joni looked at Aaron. 'Are you OK?'

'Sure.'

But clearly his sangfroid didn't fool her. 'It's the same type of malaria your brother had, and Nick's only a year younger than Ned was. The case must be bringing it back to you.'

It was. He shrugged. 'I'm fine. But thank you for asking.'

'I guess,' she said softly. 'Aaron, I know you hate talking about things. But sometimes it helps to unload to someone else instead of bottling it up. If you ever want to talk, I'm here. Even if it's stupid o'clock in the morning.'

She'd do that for him? He was stunned. Nobody had ever offered him that before.

But, then, nobody in his life had been anything like Joni. And he also hadn't let anyone as close as her, not since Ned's death. 'Thank you,' he said.

'I mean it. I'm not going to pressure you to talk, because that isn't fair. But I'm here if you need me.' Her eyes were full of sincerity, and he knew she really meant it. She really was there for him.

Suddenly not caring who saw, he slid his arms round her and hugged her. 'Thank you, Joni. I appreciate it.'

She looked utterly shocked by his unexpected display of emotion—but then she smiled and stroked his face. 'I know.' And the expression in her eyes told him that she was warmed all the way through by the fact that he'd hugged her in public.

The more time Aaron spent with Joni, the more he realised that he was falling for her. She complemented him, filled all his empty spaces. And he knew she could give him everything he'd always wanted: a close family and someone to love, who'd also love him all the way back.

Was he going to be good enough for her, though? Or would he end up disappointing her, the way he'd disappointed everyone else in his life—including himself?

He wanted to make the effort. So, the following weekend, he called over to her flat. They'd both been on duty the previous day, and hadn't had a chance to go out; he knew that she spent Sunday afternoons with her family, but he thought he might be able to snatch a few minutes with her in the morning before she had to leave to see them.

She answered the doorbell at first ring and smiled when she saw him. 'Aaron! I wasn't expecting to see you today. Come in and have a cup of tea.'

'Thanks. I'd like that.' He brought his hands from behind his back and presented her with the bouquet he'd bought. 'For you.'

'Sunflowers—how lovely!' She smiled and kissed him. 'Thank you so much.'

'I hoped you'd like them. I remembered what you said about the Van Gogh paintings.'

'And the real things are even better. I love the colour. They're so cheerful.' She beamed at him. 'I'll just put them in water. Come in.'

But as he stepped inside the door he could hear people talking. 'You have company?'

'My family,' she said. 'We take it in turns to host lunch. It's my turn today.'

It hadn't even occurred to him that they'd meet at her flat. On the rare occasions he saw his family, it was always at his parents' home. He took a step back. 'Sorry. I'm intruding on your time with your family.'

'Of course you're not. Come and join us,' she said. 'And you're very welcome to stay for lunch, if you're free—because my flat's so small, I tend to do a buffet rather than a Sunday roast, and there's more than enough food to go round.'

The wariness must have shown in his expression because she reached up and kissed him again. 'Stop thinking and come in. If you want to make yourself useful, you can make some coffee.'

He was relieved to have a job to do—and to have a respite from facing her family, even though it was only a small one. It wasn't that he disliked them—he'd responded to their warmth and friendliness when he'd met them at the concert—but this was way outside his comfort zone. And even having Joni by his side wasn't enough to stem the panic that this was all going to go horribly wrong.

'Something smells nice,' he said, trying to distract himself.

'Nothing too exciting, I'm afraid,' she said. 'I made ratatouille earlier, the jacket potatoes are doing now, and I'll put the salmon and chicken in the oven a bit later.'

'I feel bad about not contributing.'

'That's my fault for inviting you at the very last second—anyway, you brought me flowers. That counts as a contribution.' She kissed him again. 'Stop fussing and make the coffee.'

'Yes, ma'am,' he said, wishing he was a hundred miles away right now. He didn't feel anywhere near ready for this. To meet her family as her partner, not just as her colleague.

He made a pot of coffee, then followed her in to the living room. Sam and Marianna were there, along with Luke and Olly and their girlfriends; they all greeted him warmly.

Aaron did his best to be friendly and polite and fit in, the way he always did, but inside he felt such a fake. These people were all such a close unit, and he just didn't belong here—just as he didn't really belong in his own family. And he knew the fault was in him, not them.

So he had the answer to his question after all. He couldn't be enough for Joni. She deserved more than he could give her. And, even though he was willing to try his best, he knew that you couldn't be more than the sum of your parts. He couldn't be someone he wasn't. Someone who was good at emotional stuff, who could connect on a deeper level with her family and her friends, who could make her feel that she was the centre of the universe.

He couldn't do any of that.

Yes, the physical attraction between them was strong. Yes, he liked her—more than liked her. This was as close as he'd ever got to falling in love. But he couldn't be the man she needed. And the longer he let their relationship go on, the more hurt both of them would be when it ended. So he needed to stop it now. He wouldn't break up with her in front of her family—he wasn't that crass—but he'd find a quiet moment tomorrow. And then he'd do the right thing. For both their sakes.

Later that evening, after Aaron had left, Marianna said, 'He's quite cagey, isn't he, your Aaron?'

'How do you mean, Mum?' Joni asked.

'He doesn't give away anything about himself, does he? Don't get me wrong, he seems a sweetie and he's polite and charming, but...' She shook her head. 'Every time I asked him something personal, he changed the subject. I mean, I work with young children. I know all the distraction techniques. And he was definitely using them on me.'

'Mum, we haven't been together long, and he didn't know you were all going to be here today—I did rather drop him in at the deep end,'

Joni said. 'Meeting you as my partner isn't quite the same as meeting you as my colleague.'

'Even so. I can't put my finger on it, but something isn't quite right,' Marianna said, sounding concerned. 'It worries me.'

Joni hugged her. 'That's because you're my mum and you're *supposed* to worry. It's fine. Just early days, that's all. His family are all in the army, so I guess he's used to not getting too close to people because he was never in one place for that long when he was younger. And he went to boarding school when he was quite young. I guess that would make anyone a bit reserved.'

'Maybe.' But Marianna didn't look convinced.

'He's not like Marty.' Joni smiled at her. 'Don't worry, Mum. It's all going to be just fine.'

On Monday morning, Aaron caught up with Joni in the staff kitchen just before clinic. 'We need to talk,' he said quietly. 'Can we meet in the canteen after clinic?'

'Sure,' Joni said.

But he looked grim, and she had a nasty feeling that things were just about to go completely pear-shaped. Especially as Aaron had made an excuse to leave before her family had, the day before—and he hadn't called her or texted her later that evening. She'd thought maybe he was panicking a bit about meeting her family and needed some space to come to terms with it; or maybe she'd done completely the wrong thing and given him too much time to brood and come to the wrong conclusion.

But her clinic was totally full that morning and she was so rushed off her feet that she didn't have time to think about the situation and work out how to fix things.

When she met Aaron in the canteen, he said, 'Maybe we can grab a sandwich and head to the park?'

'Sure,' she said, giving him a bright smile, but she was feeling worse and worse about this. As if there was a black hole in her heart, sucking everything in and leaving a vacuum.

He waited until they were out of earshot of everyone in the park before he spoke. 'Joni, I'm sorry. This thing between us…'

He was ending it. Which she'd half expected,

but it still hurt. They'd been getting on so well. Everything had been fine.

Until yesterday, when he'd gone really quiet on her.

When he'd spent the afternoon with her family.

So it looked as if she'd made the same mistake all over again: she'd let herself fall for a man who wasn't comfortable with his family and was even less comfortable with the fact that she was close to hers.

What an idiot she'd been, thinking that at last she'd found someone who cared about her for who she was, not for who he wanted her to be. So much for taking off her rose-tinted glasses. She hadn't done that at all; if anything, she'd let them become blinkers.

OK. She could let him end it—or she could keep her pride intact and be the one to end it. Either way it would hurt like hell, but at least being the one to call a halt would make her feel slightly less inferior. She lifted her chin. 'You're right,' she said, trying to sound and cool and breezy and professional as she could. 'It's too complicated, with us being colleagues. It's probably best to stick to just working with each other. Take out the personal stuff.'

He looked relieved that she wasn't going to make a fuss. 'I'm sorry.'

That was her line. Not that she could quite bear to make a joke about it.

But he shouldn't be apologising because it wasn't just his fault, was it? It was hers, too, for being so stupid. For thinking that maybe they could have a future. For thinking that he might feel the same way about her as she felt about him. For not learning from her past mistakes. 'Not a problem.' She gave him her brightest smile. 'Actually—I don't really have time for lunch. I have a horrendous amount of paperwork that I really should catch up with. So I'll see you later, OK?'

And she left before he could say another word. Before her smile stopped being able to mask how hurt and miserable she felt. And she was never, ever going to let herself fall in love again.

Aaron felt hideously guilty as Joni walked away from him, knowing that he'd hurt her. But he was absolutely sure that he'd done the right thing, for her sake. Even though it hurt him, too. Right at the start, he'd said to her that if he were different he'd ask her out. Although she'd believed that he could be different, it turned out that he couldn't after all. So it was definitely better to end it now.

Though having Joni at arm's length in his life, a colleague rather than his lover, meant that everything felt faded. All the brightness was gone. For the first time ever, Aaron recognised exactly what he'd been feeling all those years—a feeling that had gone away while he'd been seeing Joni, but now was firmly back in place.

Loneliness.

Well, tough. He'd just have to live with it. Because feeling miserable and lonely was a damn sight better than making *her* feel miserable and lonely. And he'd done the right thing. He really had. He'd given her the chance to find someone who deserved her.

CHAPTER THIRTEEN

FOR THE NEXT week, work was grim. Aaron just kept out of Joni's way as much as possible, and buried himself in paperwork in between clinics and ward rounds. And he most definitely didn't go on the next team night out. He knew he'd have to show up at the one after that, because he'd organised it, but he just couldn't face seeing Joni outside work. Not until he'd got his feelings completely under control and had managed to stop himself wanting to hold her every time he saw her. Not until he'd forced himself to stop missing her.

The whole thing was ridiculous. He knew it wasn't going to work out between them and he'd just make her miserable. So why couldn't he stop being so selfish? Why couldn't he stop wanting her? And why couldn't he ignore the growing urge to tell her that he'd just made the biggest mistake of his life and ask her to give him another chance?

Luckily she had a couple of days off that didn't coincide with his own off-duty. Having a bit of space between them was good. It might even help his head get with the programme.

Except it didn't.

He missed her more than ever.

And the only thing that saved him was the fact that they were really, really busy in the department. Although he was rostered onto the same clinics as Joni, she didn't ask for his advice with any of her cases, and he didn't need to consult her about any of his. Even though he did think about it when Mrs Moore came in.

'So you've been having flu-like symptoms for a few days,' he said, making notes.

'I've been hot and cold, and then I got this annoying dry cough and I started bringing up this disgusting greeny-yellow stuff. And it's really hard to breathe.' She bit her lip. 'I wouldn't have bothered a doctor with it, but there was a bit of blood whenever I brought something up, so I panicked a bit.'

'Sometimes coughing can burst some of the tiny blood vessels, and that's why you see blood when you have a productive cough. It's very common,' Aaron reassured her. 'You've obviously got an infection, so if you don't mind me taking a blood sample I can do some tests to pin it down and give you the right treatment for it.'

'Thank you, Doctor. It's so *stupid* getting the flu when you've been away in the sun,' Mrs Moore said.

'Where did you go?' Aaron asked, partly to be polite and partly to help distract his patient while he took the blood sample.

'Spain. Though it wasn't quite what we were hoping for—the food wasn't so good, and the air-conditioning at the hotel was on the blink half the time.'

Alarm bells rang in the back of Aaron's head. 'Did you go on your own, or with friends?'

'With friends—there were a couple dozen of us. We went for a wedding, and we all stayed on together.'

'Do you know if any of the others have come down with the same kind of symptoms?'

She thought about it. 'Yes, actually, a couple of them have.'

'There's a possibility,' Aaron said, 'that you have Legionnaires' disease.'

'Legionnaires' disease?' Mrs Moore asked.

'It's caused by a bacterium that spreads in water.'

'So I might have caught it and given it to my friends?'

He shook his head. 'It doesn't spread between people and you don't get it by drinking contaminated water—you get it from breathing in drops of contaminated water in the air. Air-conditioning's one of the main causes—often the system's got a bit of limescale or rust in it, and that gives the bacteria the chance to grow.'

'Oh, my God.' She blew out a breath. 'We all thought the hotel wasn't brilliant. And now it's made us ill.'

'I'd like you to give me a urine sample,' he said, 'so I can test you for Legionnaires'. And if it's positive, I need you to get in touch with your friends for me and ask them to come in for testing and treatment. It's a notifiable disease,

270 of STARTED WITH NO STRINGS…

so I'll need the hotel name as well so I can talk to the public health authority in Spain.'

'Of course,' she said.

Aaron saw Joni in the corridor in between clinics. She looked pale and drawn, so he guessed that she was doing the same as he was—throwing herself into work to try and block out how she felt about the situation, and not sleeping properly.

But did she regret their break-up as much as he did? Did she wonder if they could make it work if they gave it another chance—if they could manage to put their past behind them and try again?

There was only one way to find out.

And it scared the hell out of him, because it was taking a huge risk. Getting involved. Admitting how he really felt about her. Facing up to his emotions. Knowing that she could say no and walk away.

He just needed to find the right words.

On his break, he stayed in his office rather than grabbing a cold drink in the staff kitchen.

He looked up something on the Internet that he hoped might make Joni realise that he was serious about this. As soon as their shift finished, he planned to find her. Ask her to talk. And then he'd tell her what was in his heart. If she said no…well, he'd have to live with that and know it was his own fault for messing things up. But if he had the courage to ask, then maybe, just maybe, that would give her the courage to say yes.

Mrs Moore's test came back positive.

'It's definitely Legionnaires',' Aaron told her. 'I'm going to give you some antibiotics to clear it up, but I'm also going to send you for an X-ray to check your lungs, especially as you've been coughing up blood and you've had a hard time breathing.'

'Will I have to stay in?' She looked worried. 'Only I have my diabetic review with the practice nurse on Friday.'

'That really depends on the X-rays, but as you have diabetes I'd like to keep a closer eye on you—as you probably already know, diabetes

makes you a bit more vulnerable to infections,'
he said. And if only Joni was here to reassure
Mrs Moore, to talk to her as a fellow diabetic.
Yet again he missed her, as a colleague as well as
a partner. 'Legionnaires' basically makes the tissues of your lungs inflamed so they don't work
as well and your oxygen levels drop a bit,' he
explained, 'so I'd quite like you to stay in for a
couple of days and give you some oxygen treatment as well, just so you don't have to struggle
so much.' He smiled at her. 'Try not to worry.
You'll start to feel better in a couple of days,
once the antibiotics have started working, and
the oxygen will help. It might take a couple of
weeks until you're totally back to normal, and
you can expect to feel really tired until then, but
you'll be fine.'

Aaron left his office door open at the end of his
shift while he finished off his paperwork, keeping one eye out for Joni. He'd just finished and
walked into the corridor when he saw her.

'Joni, can I have a quick—?' he began—
but when she turned towards him, the colour

drained out of her face and she keeled over in front of him.

'Joni? Joni?'

Collapsing in a faint like that wasn't good. Especially given her medical history.

Oh, hell. Please, please don't let anything happen to her.

Trying to ignore the panic rushing through his veins, Aaron went over to her and knelt down beside her to check her airways, breathing and circulation. Be a doctor first, he reminded himself. Once Joni was safe, he could let his emotions out. But right now she needed him to be a doctor. To be the best he could be.

She was breathing and her airways didn't seem compromised, but she was definitely unconscious. Aaron knew she was usually meticulous about controlling her diabetes, but he thought it was worth checking her blood sugar. If she hadn't been sleeping properly and had been working crazy hours, she might have been too distracted to keep a proper eye on her blood-sugar levels.

Nancy came rushing over. 'What's happened?'

'She just passed out in front of me.' Aaron cradled Joni in his lap. 'We need to check her blood sugar.'

'She keeps her kit in her bag. I'm sure she won't mind me looking for it.' Nancy quickly found the blood-sugar testing kit, and Aaron pricked Joni's finger and tested the blood on the strip.

'She's having a hypo,' he said. 'Her blood sugar's way too low. She's unconscious so I can't give her oral glucose in case she chokes on it. I need to give her intramuscular glucagon.'

Nancy looked grim. 'There's a kit on the medication trolley. I'll get it.'

'Can you bring a cloth and some water too, please?' he asked. Then he turned to Joni. 'Hang on in there, Nizhoni who lives up to her name. We'll sort this. And then—well, then I hope you'll give me another chance.' He stroked her hair out of her eyes. She looked so fragile, so vulnerable.

'And I swear I'll never let anything hurt you again,' he said softly.

Nancy returned with the glucagon kit and

water. Aaron mixed up the solution and drew it up into a syringe.

'Help me put her in the recovery position before I do this,' he said to Nancy. Administering glucagon could cause some diabetics to vomit, and the last thing Joni needed when she came round was to start choking.

Once she was safely on her side, he picked up the syringe and injected the solution into the muscle of her upper arm. Hopefully it would take effect quickly.

'If she doesn't regain consciousness within the next ten minutes, we need to recheck her blood sugar,' he said to Nancy, 'then give her a second dose of glucagon and get her straight to the emergency department.'

'I'll get a trolley bed in case we need to take her down,' she said.

He stayed with Joni, checking her breathing and her pulse.

Please let the glucagon work quickly. Please let it be enough so she'd recover and wouldn't need emergency treatment.

Just as Nancy came back with the wheeled

bed, Joni's eyes fluttered open. The next second, she threw up everywhere.

'Oh, no. I'm so sorry,' she mumbled.

'Don't apologise. It's not your fault,' he said, and cleaned her up.

'I feel terrible.' She groaned. 'What happened?'

'You passed out,' he said. 'You had a hypo.'

'But I—'

'Shh. Don't try to talk, not yet. You need to recover. And the reason you threw up is because of me—your blood sugar was way too low and you were unconscious, so I couldn't risk putting glucose gel in your mouth or anything.'

'You gave me glucagon?' she asked.

He nodded. 'Your arm might be a bit sore tomorrow. Sorry.'

'Better a sore arm than diabetic coma,' she said groggily.

'Take a sip of water. It'll make your mouth feel better.' He offered her the cup. 'Nancy, if you want to get off, I'll finish up here,' he said.

'Are you sure?' the nurse asked.

'I'm sure.' More sure than he'd been of anything else in his life.

'I'll take the trolley bed back on my way out,' she said.

'Thanks.' He got to his feet, lifted Joni in his arms, and carried her down the corridor.

'Where are we—?' she began.

'My office. So you can sit down and recover for a bit before you even think about going home,' he said. 'Doctor's orders.'

'Bossy.' But at least she was smiling. That was a good sign—wasn't it?

Once in his office, he didn't want to let her go. He wanted to keep her safely in his arms. But he knew he didn't have the right. Not yet. So he gently set her down in his chair. 'I'll get you some more water,' he said, 'and something to eat from the vending machine. Will a cereal bar do if there aren't any sandwiches left?'

'Anything with some slow-release carbs,' she said, sounding tired. 'Thank you.'

'Don't go to sleep. Don't move. If you feel faint, put your head between your knees.'

When he came back with a couple of cereal bars, some more water and some mints to make her mouth feel fresher, she was still sitting there, looking a bit dazed.

'Thank you. I think you just saved my life,' she said.

He shrugged. 'You had a hypo and I gave you glucagon.'

'I passed out. My blood sugar must've been...'

'Way too low. I know. I tested it,' he said. 'Eat, and then talk.'

She ate one of the cereal bars, sipped the water and then ate one of the mints. 'Thank you. You've really looked after me.'

Because I love you, Aaron thought, and I don't want to be without you, and seeing you unconscious brought the whole thing into sharp focus. But he wasn't going to dump that on her just yet. He needed to use the right words. 'I was hardly going to leave you on the floor, collapsed,' he said. 'You're normally meticulous about your blood sugar. What happened? Have you had some kind of bug or something?'

'I've been feeling a bit odd for a day or two,' she admitted. 'I had a couple of days off earlier in the week.'

He knew. He'd missed her. Horribly.

'I didn't rush around or anything. I'd been feeling a bit sweaty and shaky, but I thought it was just one of the summer bugs doing the rounds. I thought I was OK today.' She grimaced. 'I should've kept a closer eye on my blood sugar.'

'We've been really busy on the ward,' he said, 'so while you've been here you've been rushing around. And the stress I caused you didn't help.'

She looked wary. 'We're not talking about that. It's personal stuff.'

'Which is exactly why we need to talk about it.'

She frowned. 'You don't do personal, Aaron.'

'Past tense. It's time I learned how,' he said. 'Because, since we broke up, I've been totally miserable. And I've realised how wrong and how stupid I've been. I was going to ask you if we could talk, before you collapsed.'

'Uh-huh.' She looked wary.

'My timing's rubbish. And you already know I'm totally slow on the uptake,' he said. 'But seeing you unconscious like that really brought it home to me—it made me think of what life would be without you. And it…it's unbearable.'

'But—we agreed we'd just be colleagues.'

'That's not enough for me,' he said. 'I made the biggest mistake of my life, pushing you away like that. And there's something I really need to say to you, Joni. As well as sorry for hurting you.' He took a deep breath. 'Ay-oo—oh, hell.'

'"Ay-oo—oh, hell"?' she repeated, looking totally confused. 'Have I lost the plot or are you talking gibberish at me?'

'I'm trying… I practised this and I was so sure I'd got it. And now I can't think straight. I can't remember the words. Seeing you there, not moving—it's scrambled my brain. Wait.' He grabbed his phone and sifted through the notes he'd made earlier. 'Right. Nizhoni Parker, ah-yoh ah-nee-nish-neh,' he said slowly.

She looked at him, stunned. 'Did you just say what I think you did?'

'I hope I got the pronunciation right. I looked it up on half a dozen videos.' Navajo wasn't exactly the easiest language to learn. 'And I wrote it down to remind me.'

She smiled. *'Ayóó ánííníshní.'*

It didn't sound quite the same as it had when he'd said it. 'So I got it wrong?'

'No. You got it right.' She stared at him. 'I can't believe you just said that to me. And in Navajo.'

I love you. It wasn't something he'd ever said to anyone before.

'I wanted to make the effort, and I wanted you to *know* that I'm making the effort, which is why I said it in Navajo instead of English,' he said. 'Because you said that's been the problem in the past. You've always picked the wrong guy—the one who's too selfish or too lazy to try. The one who always makes you feel that he's not as into you as you are into him. And I include me in that, because I really messed up. I hurt you, and I apologise.'

He blew out a breath. 'I'm not good at emotional stuff. I've spent my whole life doing the stiff upper lip thing. I've got three generations before me who did exactly the same. So I'm probably going to need reminders to act like a normal person and actually say what I feel. But

I promise you I'll try from now on. And I want to put as much effort into this as you have. I want to make you feel the same way about me as I feel about you.'

She said nothing, but he knew she was just giving him the space to talk and not crowding him—because her expression was suddenly full of hope.

'I love you,' he said. 'Ah-yoh ah-nee-nish-neh. It scares the hell out of me, but it's how I feel and I can't stop it, even though I've tried. I'm a better man when I'm with you. But my family— they're not like yours. They're not close. I make a duty call to my parents once a fortnight, but we never talk for more than a couple of minutes. If they ask me how I am, they expect the answer to be "Fine"—so in their view the question doesn't really need to be asked in the first place.'

She laid her palm against the flat of her cheek. 'That's hard for you.'

'Not really. I'm used to it. It's how I grew up.' He shrugged. 'And it's the same with my sister and my other brother.'

She blinked. 'I didn't even know you had another brother and a sister.'

'They're both older than Ned. My parents spaced their children two years apart—except for me.' He flapped a dismissive hand. 'I guess accidents happen.'

She stared at him, shocked. 'You think they didn't want you?'

'They didn't *plan* me,' he corrected. 'As for wanting…it's all to do with the stiff upper lip. You just get on with things and you don't whine about the situation.'

'Right. So your brother and your sister…?'

'Sally's in Africa and Ben's in the Middle East. They're both in the armed forces, too. And they all think I wussed out, working in a safe hospital in England instead of being a battlefield doctor.' He blew out a breath. 'We have almost nothing in common and I can't even remember the last time we were all together. We're really not close. It's not a problem for me—I've never known any different. But it worries me that it'll hurt you, because that's not how it is for you.'

'So my family must've felt really full on for

you.' She looked anxious. 'Too much to cope with. That's why you left early—why you backed away the day after.'

'Your family's lovely,' he said. 'They're warm and caring and supportive. But.' He had to face it. 'I can't live up to them, Joni.'

'You don't need to live up to anyone,' she said. 'All you need to do is be yourself.'

He tried to suppress it, not wanting to sound needy, but the question burst out anyway. 'How do you know that's going to be enough for you?'

'Because I know what I need,' she said.

Hope began to bloom. 'Which is?'

'Someone who enjoys quirky stuff. Someone who makes great coffee. Someone who makes me feel that the sun's shining even when there's a storm blowing outside.'

That was how he made her feel? Or was that was she wanted him to be?

The question must have been written all over his face, because she said softly, 'I need *you*, Aaron. Just as you are.'

'There's a huge gulf between the way you are and the way I am. I'm rubbish at all the emotional stuff.'

'If you're bright enough to be a consultant at the age of thirty-three, then you're also bright enough to learn about emotional stuff. With the right teacher. Which,' she said, 'would be me.'

'I want to be different,' he said softly. 'But we've been here before. I tried. I was a disappointment.'

'Not to me, you weren't. Well.' She wrinkled her nose. 'It was pretty bad when I realised you were going to dump me.'

'I disappointed myself,' he said. 'I'm not enough for you.'

'You've spent your whole life thinking you're not enough,' she said softly. 'And yet look at you. If you weren't enough, you wouldn't have qualified as a doctor. You wouldn't be a consultant at such a young age. You wouldn't get cute little hand-drawn thank-you cards from our younger patients.'

'That's different.' He flapped a dismissive hand. 'It's work. That's fine.'

'Work is part of who you are,' she said. 'And if you weren't enough, I wouldn't feel the way I do about you. I wouldn't feel brave enough to want to take the risk of spending my future with you.'

'You'd take that risk?' He looked at her, shocked.

'Yes. Because I love you, too, Aaron. I admit, it started out as something different, when you asked me to dance with you. It was just physical stuff. But the more I've got to know you—both in and out of work—the more I've grown to like you. And it's not just like.' She stroked his face. 'And you've told me how you feel about me. You really mean that?'

'I really mean that,' he said. 'I've never felt like this about anyone before. I've always kept myself apart. But you—you're like sunshine. Irresistible. You make my world brighter just by being there.' He paused. 'I can't promise you a perfect life.'

'Nobody can make a promise like that,' she said. 'It's just setting yourself up for failure. So we're not going to promise each other perfection. But we can promise to stand by each other. To be there when we need each other. To listen. Maybe to argue some sense into each other from time to time.'

He smiled then. 'Is that what you're doing to me right now?'

She smiled back. 'Pretty much.'

'Maybe you're right.'

She coughed.

'*Probably* you're right,' he amended. 'And you'll probably have to talk sense into me quite a bit.'

'I can live with that.'

'If you're brave enough to take the risk,' he said, 'then so am I.'

'Together.' She took his hand.

'Together,' he echoed, and folded his fingers round hers. 'Nizhoni Parker, I can't promise you a perfect life. But I do promise to love you for the rest of my days. And, with you by my side, I'll be a better man.'

'You're already good enough for me,' she said. 'And maybe I'll just have to tell you that every single day, until you start believing it for yourself.' She paused. '*Ayóó ánííníshní.*'

'Ah-yoh ah-nee-nish-neh. I love you, too,' he said.

* * * * *

MILLS & BOON®
Large Print Medical

May

PLAYING THE PLAYBOY'S SWEETHEART	Carol Marinelli
UNWRAPPING HER ITALIAN DOC	Carol Marinelli
A DOCTOR BY DAY...	Emily Forbes
TAMED BY THE RENEGADE	Emily Forbes
A LITTLE CHRISTMAS MAGIC	Alison Roberts
CHRISTMAS WITH THE MAVERICK MILLIONAIRE	Scarlet Wilson

June

MIDWIFE'S CHRISTMAS PROPOSAL	Fiona McArthur
MIDWIFE'S MISTLETOE BABY	Fiona McArthur
A BABY ON HER CHRISTMAS LIST	Louisa George
A FAMILY THIS CHRISTMAS	Sue MacKay
FALLING FOR DR DECEMBER	Susanne Hampton
SNOWBOUND WITH THE SURGEON	Annie Claydon

July

HOW TO FIND A MAN IN FIVE DATES	Tina Beckett
BREAKING HER NO-DATING RULE	Amalie Berlin
IT HAPPENED ONE NIGHT SHIFT	Amy Andrews
TAMED BY HER ARMY DOC'S TOUCH	Lucy Ryder
A CHILD TO BIND THEM	Lucy Clark
THE BABY THAT CHANGED HER LIFE	Louisa Heaton